I0585484

Hard Road Home

Susanne Bellamy

Copyright © 2018 Susanne Bellamy

All rights reserved.

978-0-6484569-3-3

DEDICATION

For Steve - thank you for loving me, and for your support and encouragement and patience.

ACKNOWLEDGMENTS

As always, many thanks to my editor and critique partner, Annie Seaton, for her support, enthusiasm and guidance, and to Caitlin Rees and Erin Moira O'Hara for critiques and proof reading. You make my work shine!

Chapter One

"Why?" Geilis Romney couldn't prevent the shock spilling from her lips in one explosive syllable.

Her father's eyes widened and he gripped the arm of the chair with his good hand. "Why— as in why hire anyone to help you run the vineyard, or why hire Rick Peyton?"

Gei's mind grappled with the alternatives, neither of which pleased her. The first suggested arrogance on her part to expect her father to hand over total control, but the second . . . why did the fact he'd chosen Rick bother her so much? "You asked me to step in and run the vineyard while you're recuperating and then you went behind my back and hired . . . someone. Damn it, of all people you could have hired, why Rick Peyton?"

"Geilis Maree Romney, never tell me you've caught the small-mindedness of some people around here? I'm disappointed that you *of all people*"—God, she hated it when he copied her words in that tone of voice—"can't see the value in giving a man like Rick another chance now he's out of prison."

"But it's not—" Biting off her response she turned and looked out over the sea of grapevines laden with ripening bunches. Gently curving rows followed the slope down towards Lark Creek. Outside the work shed their field workers waited for her father to assign their jobs for the day. Harvest time was fast approaching and the lack of rain had produced more intense sugar in the fruit, developing a flavour she was certain would result in their best vintage in several years.

Movement along the top row of vines caught her eye. Rick stopped near the end of the row and looked around as though checking the area. What was he looking for? A muscled forearm pushed his battered Akubra up before he dropped to one knee and examined the fruit.

Gei huffed out a breath that fogged the window, briefly obscuring Rick. Antipathy towards the hired help wouldn't make managing the family business easier. Explaining her objections to her father was impossible, when she didn't fully understand the *why* of it herself. It hurt that Dad believed her capable of such petty behaviour, but why couldn't he see Rick's presence as a potential stumbling block to their plans for the winery? For goodness sake, they weren't a charity, and the name of Rick Peyton was mud in Lark Creek.

"Do you really think employing a man just out of jail for stealing from people who live in Lark Creek is good for Romney Wines' image, Dad?"

"He's paid a high price for what happened and he's had the guts to come back and face the community. I think he deserves a second chance. Don't you?"

She glanced at her father before turning back to observe Rick. In what world did he deserve a second chance? Good people didn't go around stealing from friends.

Bad people don't help out their neighbours like Rick had helped Merle and Bessie and other elderly widows in town.

Underneath his slow smile and watchfulness, was Rick good or bad? Even before he had been found guilty, he'd unsettled her. Coming home from uni with some level of maturity and an oenology degree under her belt, the sight of Rick up a ladder clearing Merle Leonard's gutters had momentarily stolen Geilis' ability to think and to breathe. He was a good-looking man—make that more like a feast for her eyes—and the fact he was helping Merle in a neighbourly way for no pay shot his appeal sky-high. That first sight of him after several years away at uni had rocked her.

Alarmed and shocked her.

She and Katy might have ogled Travis Roberts' poster a time or three, but Geilis wasn't really interested in the singer. But Rick Peyton—he'd sent her interest skyrocketing.

He moved further along the row and she sighed. She couldn't—wouldn't—allow herself to be distracted by his physical appeal. Rick Peyton was bad news. He'd done wrong once. In her book, that equated to a bad risk. Working with her father, Romney Wines was going to become one of Australia's top boutique wineries and no man—especially not one who'd proven to be untrustworthy—was going to come between her and her goal.

This morning, wanting to dislike Rick for the way her body reacted at even the memory of his shirtless splendour, she locked her attraction behind sarcastic comments and studied indifference. He hadn't lived up to the image she had of him.

Her gaze zeroed in on his tall, lean frame and drank its fill. The memory of Rick's toned body when he stripped off his T-shirt and dropped it while cleaning Merle's gutters superimposed itself on the scene in front of her, and her hands rose to cover her heated cheeks.

Damn the distraction and damn Rick for accepting the job here. He's bad for business.

She turned and faced her father, bracing for an argument. Morning light slanted through the east-facing window highlighting grey in his hair she'd never noticed before. Her heart thudded as she realised his shoulders had developed a stoop seemingly overnight. Guilt lodged like a ball of lead in her stomach. She had come too close to losing her father to risk his health now. In his weakened state, he couldn't work in the vineyard, but he'd hired Rick to provide the muscle. How could she add to his concerns by refusing to accept Rick Peyton?

Biting her tongue for the few weeks Rick would be employed couldn't be that difficult. And keeping a close eye on him offered the minor compensation of a reason to watch him at work.

Was that a silver lining, or yet one more problem?

Fixing a smile in place, she patted her father's shoulder. "It won't be a problem, Dad. Rick is here for a limited time as the muscle. When your arm has healed, he'll be gone and we'll be back to the way we were."

God, she hoped they could go back to the way they were. Because if Rick Peyton's presence caused one iota of negative publicity, she would personally kick him into Lark Creek.

***

Rick looked over the rows of grape vines angling down the slope towards Lark Creek and wondered what the hell he'd agreed to. White grapes hung in small, plump bunches on his left, and off to the right, heavy, dark purple orbs clung to vines. They looked ripe and ready for the picking, but what did he know about wine? Before he'd been sent to prison he rarely drank anything other than an amber brew.

He shrugged and climbed onto the quad bike. Not that his taste in drink mattered. Thanks to Reg, he had a job doing the heavy lifting at Romney wines. For an ex-con, landing a job was a big step.

Ex-con. Gritting his teeth, he tipped his head back and looked at the wide arc of open sky. Unimpeded by cold bars and barbed wire, it disappeared beyond the far hill where he could make out Travis' house at Thornyhill Farm. Below the edge of the vineyard, the creek meandered and, in the still summer air, the sound of water trickling over rocks at the bend

4

carried to his ears. If he wanted, he could stroll down to the bank and spend as much time as he needed simply sitting and watching the creek. Toss in a stick, skim a few stones—*think.* No rules, no strictly regulated outside time—nothing but nature inviting him to disappear into the bush and sleep under the stars.

Six months jail time, six months behind bars and forever labelled a criminal.

Had his sacrifice been enough to prevent his brother from further crimes?

Rick closed his eyes and drew in a deep lungful of air. The scent of earth and ripening fruit on the vine filled his nostrils.

The scent of freedom.

"If you're going to waste our time daydreaming, get off that quad bike and let me take the equipment to the lower section."

His eyelids flew open at the annoyed tone. Geilis Romney stood on the bluestone patio looking down at him, arms folded across her waist and a no-nonsense *hiring-you-was-a-mistake* expression in her eyes. She was all business. Her red-checked shirt was knotted at her waist and a pair of faded denims disappeared into the tops of work boots. A battered, broad-brimmed hat lay on the ironwork table next to her. Clearly she intended to supervise him in the first task Reg had set for the day. The idea grated against Rick's newfound freedom.

Suppressing the urge to respond came automatically. Passive face, hands otherwise engaged in gripping the steering wheel—he'd quickly learned the technique of *non-involvement,* and had avoided trouble in the exercise yard. Watching without appearing to look, heightened awareness of his surroundings, and most important of all, giving away nothing of his true feelings.

Let it slide like water off a duck's back.

"On my way." He slapped his hat on his head, turned the key in the ignition and released the brake as Geilis stepped off the stone flagged patio. Okay, so maybe he had been enjoying his freedom for a few moments longer than necessary before work began, but after those months behind bars—six months of his life in exchange for protecting those he loved—it had felt like a stolen luxury.

He was aware of Geilis glaring at him as he drove past her down the central crossroad separating the top sections of the vineyard. Glaring and annoyed and definitely not liking his presence on Romney land.

Because I'm an ex-con. I'd better get used to it. She won't be the only one.

Chapter Two

Mixed feelings were unfamiliar to Geilis. She knew what she wanted; where she stood on things that mattered. Almost nothing scared her. Not hard work, and certainly not the idea of hiring a convicted criminal. Her father was wrong if he thought her attitude to their newest worker was about Rick's conviction. What worried her was community backlash against the hired black sheep.

He'd broken trust with Lark Creek, and she was angry because Rick's actions had disappointed her expectations of him. He was supposed to be a good man and yet his fraud had hurt many in town.

His broad shoulders appeared broader still beneath a khaki work shirt that strained to contain them. Confident he wouldn't physically harm anyone, his dark gaze sent a shiver down her spine and a primal, visceral response fluttered in her stomach as the quad bike headed downhill. She'd called him the muscle—and he was a good-looking man—but there was something about the expression in his eyes that belied the neutral mask of his face, the carefully controlled, toneless voice.

On my way.

"I'm not afraid of you." The words whispered from her mouth and disappeared into the blue sky. What was there to be afraid of?

Just a bleak darkness in his eyes and the way his gaze ignited a desire to . . . Do what?

Glaring at his disappearing back, she gave herself a pep talk. "Turn him into a model citizen again? Oh, for goodness sake, he's my employee. I'm in charge here and I'll tell him what to do." She rammed her hat on her head and stepped down onto the wide, shallow stone steps. Her father's voice stopped her.

"What were you muttering about, sweet pea?"

She gritted her teeth and reminded herself that Rick was here at her father's request. Fixing a smile in place, she turned to find Dad looking down at her, deep furrows etched in his brow. Her chest tightened, recalling the heart specialist's comment as he studied the X-ray. An eighty-five per cent blockage of one artery meant her darling dad could have dropped dead from a massive heart attack at any time. Good fortune had delivered him a minor incident and lifesaving stents. Worrying him with her stupid reaction to Rick wasn't going to happen. "Nothing, Dad. Just sending our newest employee about his work."

"Don't give him too hard a time, love. Be pleasant, polite, and treat him as you'd treat any other worker. Whatever bee you have in your bonnet about Rick, please give him the courtesy of a fair go."

Her father's instruction jolted her out of her funk. If he'd noticed her tension around Rick, it must be pretty obvious to anyone.

Including Rick.

She refused to give him the satisfaction of knowing he affected her in any way. Better self-control, that's what she needed. "I will, I promise. I'm going to check the grapes."

"Good girl. Harvest isn't far off. I reckon this year's vintage will be one of our best. I'm just sorry I'm not more able to help you, but Geilis?"

He looked down at her from the patio and she felt a familiar welling of love for her wonderful father. He'd never been one of those men who fussed about having no son to succeed him. Instead he'd encouraged her to try lots of activities. When she'd exhibited interest in the vineyard, he'd begun teaching her about the grapes and she'd discovered a passion for the business. "What is it, Dad?"

"I'm proud of you. You'll make a fine vintner."

"Thanks, Dad. I learned from the best."

Feeling lighter with her father's confidence tucked inside her, she strode down the central lane towards the lower terrace. A rumble of machinery indicated where Rick was carrying out the first job Dad had set him. She considered checking up on him before she went to work on her own set of tasks, but Dad's words replayed in her mind.

Fine, I'll treat him like the others and trust him. For now. But if he puts one foot out of line or draws one negative response towards our vineyard, I'll come down on him like a ton of bricks.

***

Rick walked to the end of the last row and studied the angle of the sun falling on the vines. Reg had explained the idea and process of de-leafing, and Rick figured he understood it well enough to tackle the next job on his list without Geilis hovering over his every move. He'd been aware of her keeping an eye on him from her row across the central lane. Each time he looked across, her gaze turned away as though it was pure chance she'd been looking in his direction. But every time he glanced out of the corner of his eye, he could see her surreptitiously monitoring his work.

So be it. Surely he could ignore her and imagine he was alone under the summer-blue sky, doing what he wanted to do. And yet the habits of the past six months were deeply ingrained, and his gaze slid sideways, drawn by movement and colour, needing to know precisely where she was in relation to him. Her red shirt was bright amongst the green vines, and her slim body bent and stretched in graceful, economical movements that any red-blooded male would enjoy watching.

No point going there. No hope of her softening her attitude towards me.

Geilis had made her distrust and dislike clear from the moment he'd walked into the office this morning. Back turned, stiff shoulders bristling with disapproval, she had ignored him until her father reached past her and shook Rick's hand. Geilis had quickly removed herself from the room and Reg had apologised for his daughter's cool greeting. "She's annoyed I pre-empted her and hired someone to help. Nothing personal, Rick."

It would be a miracle if it wasn't personal, but he kept his opinions to himself. "Not a problem. I'm grateful you're prepared to give me a job. I won't let you down. Hopefully Geilis will realise that too."

Maybe Reg Romney believed his daughter would change, but Rick had faced disapproval most of his life. His drunken, abusive stepfather had attracted censure for his actions and sympathy for his family from the community. There was no hiding the narrowing of eyes, or the physical distancing of bodies. He'd ended up doing the same to his stepfather and nothing would ever change his hatred of the man who'd made his childhood a misery until Rick grew tall enough and strong enough to defend himself. Then Garrett Thomas had stopped with the physical intimidation, and the only things thrown were barbed words and crude insults.

He could live with his stepfather's hatred; what he'd never be able to understand was why his mother had taken Garrett Thomas as her husband. A sweeter woman would be impossible to find.

And a nastier piece than Garrett was hard to imagine. Had he always been such a miserable man?

Rick shut down his dark memories and reminded himself of Reg's instructions. *"Only leaves facing the rising sun in the east are removed. It helps the grapes to ripen and improves aeration and it makes the task of manual harvesting much easier."*

Checking the angle of light falling on the grapes one more time, Rick snipped the stem of a leaf covering the topmost bunch of grapes. Two more snips and the bunch glowed in the late morning light, almost pearlescent. The odd thought occurred that, if grapes could feel, these were happy to feel the kiss of the sun on their green skins.

Rick snorted. It had been a long time since a fanciful thought had crossed his mind; probably since his mother had shared her love of poetry with him and taught him to appreciate the tiny details in the wonder of nature. He clamped a lid over the ache in his heart where his mother's memory remained as bright as ever. No amount of time could heal that wound.

He moved steadily along his row heading for the lane break, feeling more confident as he went.

"Who the hell told you to start cutting into the leaves?" Angry words penetrated the wall of green and Geilis' face appeared over the top of the frame. Standing on the lower side of the slope, he found himself at an unfamiliar physical disadvantage, looking up into a pair of angry green eyes.

Rick looked down, snipped the leaf in his hand and let it to flutter to the ground before he allowed his gaze to meet hers. "Your father."

"It's a specialised task. Besides, I'm doing it. Why would he ask you to do it too?"

"Probably because it needs to be finished and it's already a bit late in the season."

"But you've never done it before. You have to—"

"He explained exactly what to do. Want to check out my work so far? I've just about finished this row."

She raised an eyebrow and glared at him. "You can't have done it properly in the time you've had. Let me look." She strode around the end pole and planted her feet next to him. With an imperious tilt to her head she examined the last plant he'd trimmed. A ridge settled between her brows as she moved on to the next plant, her hand gently brushing the leaves surrounding the grapes. By the time she'd moved on to the neighbouring plant, she was nodding her head.

Satisfaction filled him, and he folded his arms as Geilis moved to the far end of his row, checking each vine. She snipped off a leaf from the second plant he'd worked on and strolled back to where he waited.

"Hmph, not bad for a first attempt." Her gaze connected with his, held for the space of a heartbeat or two, and then slid back to the far end where he'd begun. "Okay, keep going. See if you can keep up with me, but mind you don't nick any of the fruit."

"Sure, boss. And I won't cut any either."

"What?"

"I won't cut the fruit and I promise not to nick—steal any."

"I didn't mean—" Beneath her lightly tanned skin, a hint of pink rose along her high cheekbones. She'd tossed out enough veiled insults at him. Served her right being put on the back foot for once.

Her face tilted up and she looked directly at him. One thing about Geilis Romney, she said exactly what she thought. It was annoying—and kind of refreshing. "I'm sorry if you thought I was implying that. I just meant to take care not to cut or bruise the fruit. This looks like it will be our best vintage in years."

"No offence taken." So, Miss High and Mighty wasn't quite as high in the instep as her behaviour this morning had led him to think. Thankful for small mercies, he gripped the secateurs and set to work on the last couple of vines in his row.

Geilis watched him complete one vine. Before she turned at the end of his row she stopped and looked back to him. "Good. Well then, we'll work alternate rows. When you finish this one, skip mine and start on the third bottom row and head back towards the fence."

"Got it. I'm odds, you're evens." They set to work, but he was aware of her whenever she worked on the row above his. Flashes of her red shirt caught his eye as he moved from vine to vine, and he finished his row one snip behind her. He strolled up two rows, pausing to look out towards the creek. The sight eased the tightness in his chest that had begun all those months ago, when he was taken into custody. He drew a deep lungful of air for what felt like the first time since Sergeant Edwards slapped the handcuffs on him and shoved him into the police car. He was free and employed. It was a good beginning.

He turned and lifted an overhanging leaf on the first vine. As Geilis passed the end of his row, he asked, "What about the fallen leaves? Do we collect them or leave them to mulch?"

"We'll collect them last thing before we finish for the day. Everything gets left neat and tidy in my vineyard."

***

By the time Geilis called for the lunchbreak, her shirt was sticking to her back and tendrils of hair clung to her damp face. Reluctant as she was to have Rick working on their vines, she had to hand it to him—he was a good worker. Sensible, quick to learn, he'd matched her row for row all the way through the first section of vines. As she took her hat off to wipe an arm across her forehead, he turned the corner and stood a short distance away.

"You look hot." He handed her a bottle of cold water.

She accepted gratefully, sneaking a second look while Rick drank from his. "It's summer. We're working outside. What else would you expect?" He, on the other hand, looked *hot*. Sweat sheened his throat, which rippled as he swallowed. And he moved with the easy grace of an athlete. Damn it, she wasn't going to notice him. She wasn't going to go there. Not with an employee and definitely not with a man she had once admired but who had let her down by committing a crime. Concentrating on removing her sweaty gloves, she turned away and tossed a comment over her shoulder. "You did well."

"Thanks. You set a cracking pace. So, after lunch will we move onto the next section? More of the same?"

She flexed her right hand, the one that felt like it still gripped the secateurs. She'd forgotten the ache and occasional cramping that came with this work. "Yes. If you're up to it."

Flicking a quick look in Rick's direction, she finally eased her hand out of the second glove and clipped her secateurs into their pouch on her utility belt. "I'll show you where to wash up and where staff have their lunch. Come on."

There was a single car in the visitors' car park as she led the way past the cellar door and through the back entrance to the kitchen. Her father's upbeat tone filtered through from the tasting room, lauding the selection of last year's wines.

Scrubbing her hands, she jerked her head in the direction of the public area. "Dad might not be able to work in the vineyard for now, but he's great with customers. He weaves the magic of the vines into an irresistible story. There aren't many who leave without at least a couple of bottles under their arms." She flicked water from her hands and grabbed a hand towel.

Rick moved in for his turn at the sink. "He's passionate about this place, and what you all produce. It shows when he talks about the vineyard and his wine."

For a newly-arrived employee, Rick's comment was observant. "You hit the nail on the head. It's his passion for Romney Wines that's got us this far."

"How far is your contribution going to take the vineyard?"

She gave him a coolly assessing look. "All the way to Best of Show in Sydney and beyond. I intend to make Romney Wines one of the top boutique wineries in the country."

Chapter Three

Rick pulled into the garage, climbed out of Travis' ute and stretched, feeling the pleasant pull of muscles well-used in the day. It was a different kind of fatigue to working out in the gym, the kind that came from an honest day's work.

Damn, it felt good. He collected the small esky and thermos Travis had loaned him and locked the ute out of habit.

At the back door he toed off his boots and deposited the mini-esky in the laundry.

"Dinner will be ready in twenty minutes. Grab a beer if you like." Travis' voice carried from the kitchen along with the aroma of—

"Is that your mum's beef casserole recipe?" Rick sniffed appreciatively as he entered the kitchen. "Surprisingly, that smells good. When did you learn to cook?"

"When I got hungry enough for something more than takeaway or baked beans in a can. Mum sent me a few simple recipes when I moved to Sydney. Don't expect a lot of variety. I cycle through half a dozen meals in a week."

"About that, I'm happy to take my turn cooking while I'm here. And thanks for the loan of your ute today. I'll walk tomorrow, though, and as soon as I save enough I'll pick up something second-hand."

Starting from scratch was the pits, but his car had been garnisheed along with his tools, after the fiasco of the false allegations against him. But it had saved Harvey from jail. Before his mother died he'd promised to always look out for his younger half-brother. Just as taking beatings for Harvey had been second nature with Garrett as a stepfather, Rick had accepted blame for Harvey's criminal activity.

Travis wiped his hands on a hand towel. Taking two cans of beer from the fridge, he tossed one to Rick. "Motorbike?"

Rick caught the can and set it on the laminate kitchen table. "I doubt I'll have enough for that in the time I'm likely to be working for Reg. No, I thought I might find a pushbike. Once I get on the river road it's an easy run."

"You're willing. Or are you in training again?"

"For the marathon? Hadn't thought that far ahead." He'd got through the last six months by not thinking of the days and nights stretching ahead of him, by not thinking of a future beckoning beyond the bars of prison. Now, there was a future and time he would have to fill. "I might manage the half marathon around Dalton by the end of March if I get stuck into training now."

"I'll have the quad out in the back paddock most of tomorrow. Take the ute if you like and call into Vacy's place at lunch. He might have something that suits you."

"Thanks. And I can cook dinner tomorrow and alternate nights if you like. Steak and veg okay?" He could ask Reg about a small advance on his pay if he found a bike in the second-hand yard.

"Great." Travis added peas to a microwave dish and put them in to cook.

Rick headed for the shower. Grateful to his friend and to the Romneys, and feeling lucky—most men who'd just left prison struggled to find work—he was almost tempted to start making plans to get his life back on track. Good behaviour in jail had its benefits. And its restrictions.

As a condition of your early release, you must report to your local police station every Wednesday.

If reporting in took longer than he expected, he'd have to make up the time elsewhere. He towel-dried his hair, pulled on a pair of stubbies and a fresh T-shirt, and followed his nose to the dining room where Travis had set two heaped plates on opposite sides of the table.

"Trav, have I thanked you for taking me in? I really appreciate it."

Travis held up one hand. "Enough, mate. We're friends and that's what friends do—look out for one another. Dig in." He loaded his fork with mashed potato, but stopped before he ate and looked at Rick—a shrewd look, knowing and compassionate at the same time. A look that turned the food in Rick's mouth to ashes. Whatever was coming, he didn't want to hear it.

"Great food. Your mum's recipe is a winner."

"Thanks. Have you been out to your mother's house yet?"

Deflection hadn't worked. Not that he expected it would hold Travis' question at bay. It was more a sign of his desperation to avoid thinking about *home*. "Nope." Rick shovelled a forkful of casserole into his mouth and avoided Trav's searching gaze. Would he ever be ready to go back to the house where his mother had died? But if he didn't, was that dishonouring her memory, and her bequest?

By the time their plates were empty, Rick accepted broaching the elephant in the room was necessary. Travis wasn't the sort to let a topic go, and who else was he going to tell if not his friend? "My stepfather made it clear he's got a gun if I show my face on *his property*. Mum said she'd made her will in favour of Harvey and me, but I lit out straight after her funeral. I couldn't bear sitting around listening to parts of her life being divided up between us and Garrett . . ."

Travis leaned back and rested his arms along the arms of the carver chair. "So go to a solicitor. Challenge his occupation of your house. Claim it back."

"Yeah, right. Just like that. Straight from jail and into a bun fight . . . Make that a gun fight. My parole would be rescinded and I'd be back in a cell faster than you can say 'Old man Muggeridge'. For all I know that might be Garrett's plan."

"Mate, you've got rights, same as other people, and for what it's worth, I know you. There's no way you committed the crime you went to prison for. What I can't figure out is why you didn't fight it."

"I had my reasons."

"I knew it! Who are you protecting?"

"No one. Let it go, Trav." Rick pushed his chair back and stood. He picked up both plates and stacked them noisily before removing them. He stepped away from the table, tossing out a question that he hoped would give him time to escape into the kitchen. "Is there dessert or didn't you ask your mother to teach you anything fancy?"

Travis' eyes narrowed and his gaze stopped Rick and pinned him to the spot. Once upon a time Rick would have given in to that unspoken demand and told Travis what he wanted to know. Prison had taught him to keep his mouth shut.

"I don't bake cakes if that's what you mean, but it just so happens Adam brought one of Katy's experiments when he came for his guitar lesson. It's on the top shelf in the fridge."

"Yum, experimental cooking. Can't wait." Rick strode into the kitchen and set the plates and cutlery in the sink. Leaning on the drainer he gripped the edge of the counter, closed his eyes and lowered his head. Nobody but Harvey could have accessed his accounts and moved money around. Nobody at home had those skills except tech-whiz Harvey, who compensated for his physical limitations with a brilliant mind.

But revealing his suspicions to *anyone* could create problems for his brother.

And how did he get such a brain from a bastard like Garrett Thomas?

Then again, Harvey looked more like Mum than Rick did. Rick assumed he took after his father.

If only my father hadn't died before I knew him.

He opened his eyes and stood, staring into the fading western sky. Whatever sacrifices he'd had to make, it was worth it to keep his promise to his mother. He'd looked after Harvey in the only way he could; by accepting punishment for his brother's crime. And he'd do it all over again if he had to.

"What's up, Rick? Couldn't face Katy's strawberry and daiquiri cake?"

Rick walked to the fridge and reached blindly for a pink confection on the top shelf. "Just looking at the sunset. Can't get enough of looking at scenery without barbed wire interrupting the view." He set the cake plate on the table and cut a couple of wedges.

Travis quietly set two small plates beside the cake and Rick slid a piece onto each one. A streak of pink frosting coated his finger and he licked it off. "There's rum in this." It was a small thing, but the taste of alcohol in the icing was unusual and dragged his mind from his dark thoughts.

"Katy likes trying out new flavours on me before serving them to her guests at the B and B. What do you think of it?" Travis took a big bite out of his slice and looked expectantly at Rick.

He bit into the cake. The delicate swirl of pink icing made him think of roses, but the taste hit his tongue like a summer cocktail. He nodded, replying around a mouthful of zinging flavours. "S'good. Really good."

"I'll tell her you approve. I'm going down there shortly, but mate—"

"What?" Rick popped the last piece of his serving into his mouth and licked his fingers.

"Talk to Jack Donaldson about your mother's house. He's a good lawyer, and totally discreet." Travis clapped a hand on Rick's shoulder and turned towards the bench. "I cooked, your turn to wash up."

"I'll think about the lawyer. And thanks for dinner. I'll do the dishes. See you in the morning."

Travis nodded before disappearing through the back door. A couple of minutes later, the sound of his motorbike engine roared past the house and faded as Travis headed down the back paddock to Katy's cottage. Rick grinned. Travis had always preferred his bike over the relative safety of four wheels.

He made a cup of coffee and carried it out onto the front veranda. Reclining in the settler's chair, he drank a mouthful and set the mug on the wooden arm. Streaks of gold outlined the hill across the creek valley and lights winked on at the Romney vineyard. It was calm and peaceful and he'd never take the right to something as simple as relaxing in the dark for granted again.

Chapter Four

Geilis withdrew the pipette from the cask and stoppered the bunghole before picking up her favourite tasting glass. She held it up to the light and then placed a white board behind it, assessing the wine's colour before swirling the wine with a practised hand.

"Well, what do you think?" Her father leaned forwards on the camping chair she'd set out for him before their tasting session began.

Geilis sniffed, closed her eyes and drew the bouquet of last year's wine into her nose. Testing, assessing, seeking the perfect descriptors. "Coming on nicely. Hints of lemongrass and peach." She sipped and allowed the wine to slide across her tongue, lingering over the finish as she tried to catch an elusive floral hint.

"A dratted nuisance that my doctor won't allow me to drink for a few weeks." Her father reached for her glass.

She raised an eyebrow and his eyes widened. "What? You don't think I'm going against doctor's orders, do you? I just want to inhale the bouquet."

The glass changed hands and her father went through the same actions she'd done. The appearance of the wine pleased him before he closed his eyes and inhaled. "You're right about lemongrass and peach, but there's something more there . . ." He swirled the wine and lifted the glass to his nose a second time. "Do you think that undertone is lavender?"

"You can smell it too?" Geilis still wasn't certain. The wine was young and suddenly she missed her father's guidance through the final stage of tasting. Because of the doctor's orders that he didn't drink, tasting fell squarely on her shoulders. "I thought I was imagining that scent."

"Relax, Gei. Tasting a developing wine should be a pleasure, not a chore."

"It's not a chore, Dad. I love doing it. I just want to do it right."

Perfection. Is that too much to ask?

That elusive ninety points plus rating that assured a winery's reputation and stellar sales; that was all she wanted. Her father had come close, but she was determined to achieve it.

"So long as you don't lose sight of other things that are important in life. Have fun along the way, spend time with your friends."

"I have fun. I see Katy and do stuff with her."

Her father raised an eyebrow and lowered his chin. "What about Anna? You were good friends all through school and now I never hear you mention her name."

"I saw her just the other week. Just before Christmas."

At a ceremony where Katy spread her grandmother's ashes. Maybe Dad was right, but how could Geilis go out and have a good time when there was so much to be done to cover his share of work in the vineyard? When the responsibility fell on her shoulders?

"Hmm." His eyes narrowed as they had been doing all too often since his accident. As though stepping back from overseeing everything had drawn his eagle-eyed attention squarely onto Geilis. "How's Rick working out?"

Her memory winged back to the morning. Watching Rick working was more distraction than she needed.

Or wanted.

She'd been so intent on keeping an eye on him that he'd almost beaten her to finish de-leafing. After her 'try to keep up' comments, it wasn't permissible and she'd scrambled to make up lost ground.

I was only watching him to be sure he did the job properly.

If she told herself that often enough, maybe she'd come to believe it. "He's okay. Plenty of muscle for the heavy lifting. Why?"

"Looked like he was keeping up with you during de-leafing with no trouble. Reckon he's got brains to match his brawn."

"He's not as good as you, Dad. No one's as good as you." She gave him a quick hug, fierce and urgent in its longing for everything to be all right. To be as it had been. "You'll be back in the vineyard soon and we'll make that award-winning wine together."

"About that . . ."

***

Lunch time wasn't ideal for shopping, but it was all he had. Rick pulled up in front of Vacy's second-hand yard. A faded, battered sign proclaiming the business belonged to Vacy and Son, clung drunkenly to the front fence by two screws. The final 's' had been scratched out after Vacy's oldest son, Frank, died. Rick barely remembered the flood that had taken Josh's older brother, but he remembered playing among piles of second, third, tenth-hand goods with Josh. Back then, their imagination had made the yard an island where pirate treasure was buried. Now, it was more junkyard than second-hand goods. Rusting piles of metal—ancient bed frames, parts of cars, farm machinery, and indistinguishable rust-red shapes—lined the chain-link fence down both sides of the ramshackle house. Beyond the sagging rear veranda, they merged into a pile of white goods that had long since lost that colour claim. But Rick didn't have the money to be fussy. So long as he found something with a solid frame, he'd make it work. He took the key from the ignition, got out of the ute and headed towards the tall, double gates. One side was open and slightly off-kilter, and the bottom corner dug into the dirt.

Vacy, whose first name had disappeared from Rick's memory, sauntered barefoot along the rutted dirt driveway. His navy work shirt was faded and oil-stained, and a frayed and ancient pair of King Gees displayed knobbly knees and skinny shanks. Small in stature, but wiry, Vacy had always talked big. As he stepped into the opening and gripped the metal gate edge, something in his expression brought Rick to a halt. A hard glint in eyes that narrowed as he met Rick's gaze.

"Hi, Vacy. I'm looking for—"

"We're closed." The gate swung shut in his face.

A sick, sinking feeling hit the pit of Rick's stomach like a runaway railway cart. "You've never closed during the day before."

"Today, we're closed." Vacy snapped a heavy-duty lock shut. His piercing gaze was filled with loathing. "Don't care what you're looking for. Even if we've got it, you ain't getting it. For you, we're closed—permanently."

The world closed in around him, stealing the air from his lungs, rooting his feet to the ground. "I . . . see." Was this how it would be if he stayed in his home town? Anger and resentment might be the least of his problems if he couldn't purchase the basics.

"Do you? You're a piece of shit. Nobody wants you here." Vacy grasped the rolled metal edge, his knuckles turning white with the force of his grip. "Do you even care what you did to all those people? To Josh?"

Rick hadn't thought it possible for his gut to hurt any more than it did, but mention of his friend twisted his stomach into breath-stealing knots. "What happened to Josh?"

"Like you don't know."

Rick struggled to force his desert-dry mouth to form words that made sense. "Is he okay?"

"When you stole that money, you stole his job, and his self-respect. The bank repossessed his car for non-payment of his loan. The only thing you can do for him now is get out of town and never come back." Vacy turned and strode back into his tumbledown house, slamming the door to emphasise his point.

Rick dragged in a breath, forcing air into lungs that felt like a giant clamp held them hostage. He shouldn't have come back. Lark Creek had barely been home since his mother died. If he slipped out of town today, nobody would miss him. With the exception of Reg Romney, nobody wanted him around.

He glanced down the road towards the town centre. At the far end of the main street, the brick fence and flagpole in front of the police station were visible. The flag gave a desultory flutter as an errant breeze caught the material.

There's someone else who doesn't want me around. Might as well get this over while I'm feeling like the shit Vacy labelled me.

Setting his shoulders back, he strode to the ute and drove up the hill. With any luck, Sergeant Edwards would be out on call. *Since when has luck been with me?*

Chapter Five

Lark Creek Police Station. Rick stopped at the low herringbone-brick fence and concentrated on dragging air into his constricted lungs. The signpost and flagpole cast heavy, dark shadows across his chest like prison bars. Memories crashed over him and his gut clenched as he stood looking into the dim interior of the police station. After his arrest he'd been brought into the ugly red-brick building and formally charged. The stale stink of the interview room hung like a grey fog around the memories of that day, and the knowing looks of Senior Sergeant Edwards as he read Rick his rights were as clear as if the officer stood in front of him. Rick dragged in a deep breath and set his foot on the concrete path as the front door opened.

Edwards stood in the doorway, his thumbs hooked into the waistband of his navy trousers and glared at Rick.

He lifted his chin and calmly met the police officer's gaze while inside, his gut roiled.

"How did they let a worthless pile of shit like you out early?"

Still smarting from the encounter with Vacy, Rick gritted his teeth. There were plenty in town who felt the same. "Good behaviour. I'm here to report in as part of my early release conditions."

"Yeah, you do that, Peyton. And while you're at it, remember I've got a spare cell out back just waiting for when you set a toe out of line. And you will. It's just a matter of time." Edwards' bulk filled the doorway, his beer belly sagging over his belt.

"I don't intend to accept your offer, Sergeant." It cost Rick all his self-control to keep his tone neutral, his expression, impassive. Never would he give Edwards a reason to lock him up again. He waited, hands loose at his sides, until the police sergeant spat into the bush next to Rick, turned and disappeared into his glass-panelled office.

The tightness in Rick's chest eased a notch. He went inside and waited at a polished wooden counter on newly-tiled flooring, a change since his arrest six months earlier. Given the population of Lark Creek was decreasing, the minor renovations surprised him.

A young female constable looked up from her keyboard and nodded to him. "I'll be with you in a moment, sir." Blonde hair scraped back in a bun, probably no more than twenty-five or –six, he wondered how she'd ended up at Lark Creek. And how long she'd last with Edwards as her superior.

"Thanks." It looked like his first report was going to be made to a junior officer. Hoping she was familiar with the process so he could get back to the vineyard and not be late, he let his gaze roam the small station without turning his head. A single sliding glance was all he needed to know. Edwards was leaning back in his chair, eyes narrowed on him like a bird of prey.

Grateful that his check in was a task far beneath Edwards' pay grade and dignity, Rick checked the time on a utilitarian analogue clock on the back wall and willed the young woman to finish her task and attend to him quickly. Beige walls and information posters began to press in on all sides. A trickle of sweat ran down his back and his lungs couldn't get enough air. He turned and focused on the streetscape beyond the front door. Out there was fresh air, sunshine and no uniforms.

The constable pushed her chair back and came to stand opposite Rick. "How can I help you, sir?" Her voice was precise, her words, clipped, but her gaze was clear and direct.

And in a ludicrous moment Rick wished it was Edwards facing him rather than the woman. Edwards knew what Rick had been charged with and believed the worst of him. But the constable—surname, Brooks according to her badge—had given him a pleasant smile as she tilted her head and waited for him to state his business. He hated the thought that her smile would vanish as soon as he declared why he was here. Hated what his decision was costing him.

I wouldn't have done things differently even if I'd known how hard this would be.

But he might have been better prepared for the stony glares and faces turned aside. He cleared his throat and met her eyes. "I'm here to report for my first check in. Rick Peyton's the name."

He watched her smile fade, but her gaze stayed steady on him until she set a tablet on the counter. Her fingers flew across a Bluetooth keyboard before she turned the screen to face him. "Fill in your details on this form. When you're finished, let me know and we'll continue from there."

She tapped away at a nearby desk computer, but he felt the weight of her supervision as he fumbled with the device. After a false start and several fat-finger typos, the process was complete. In less time than Rick expected, he was free from officialdom and back at the vineyard with a few minutes to spare. Stomach growling, he opened his esky and managed a mouthful of his sandwich before Geilis appeared in the staff lunchroom. "Where have you been?"

He swallowed, wondering at the frown creasing her forehead. "Into town. What's the problem?"

"There's a leak somewhere on the drip line. We need to find it and fix it now. Come on." She turned and strode through the door.

Rick put the lid on his esky and finished the sandwich in his hand in two bites as he followed her. His stomach rumbled in empty discontent.

Geilis' anxious pace was no match for his long strides. He caught up with her and slowed his pace as she turned down the last but one row of purple grapes. Sunlight reflected off a spurting fountain and an elongated puddle of water, a puddle that had turned the surrounding strips of short grass into a mudflow that crept like a mini volcano. It bubbled out from either side of the spurting water, and a lava flow of brown oozed over the last terrace and on to the creek below.

"Quick, it's got worse in the time it took me to come looking for you." Geilis squeezed between two posts onto the terrace above and ran to the gushing break. She felt through the muddy water and picked up the length of black plastic pipe, but there was no give in the heavy-duty plastic. Water spurted high as her movements changed the angle of the break and sunlight created a miniature burst of rainbows over her head. She ducked her head while water drenched both of them.

He touched her arm and raised his voice. "Where's the stopcock?"

She blinked away drops and shook her head. "On the southern side of the control shed."

Rick raced past the terraces up to the side of the shed. He flipped the cover off and wrenched the stopcock round and round until the gush of water through the pipes slowed and finally stopped. Taps were never turned on high for the drip lines, but this one had been fully open. Casting a searching look around the immediate area, he spied a glint within a tussock of dry grass near the back end of the shed. A silver key hanging off a matte metal skull and bones tag was caught on a twig. He picked up the key and slipped it into his pocket and then headed downhill to Geilis.

She was kneeling in the muddy puddle, fingers working along a section of black pipe as the water pressure slowed to a trickle. Her long plait fell over her shoulder and her checked shirt moulded to her body like a second skin. Beneath the early afternoon sun he imagined steam rising off her back and shoulders. Feeling more than a little hot under the collar at the sight of her slim body, he hunkered down beside her.

"Have you found anything?"

"Yes, look at this." She edged closer to him and leaned across. As she lifted the section of pipe between his knees her forearm brushed his thigh. No more than a second of contact, but her arm jolted as though she'd touched a live wire. Wide eyes connected, meshed with his. Awareness sharpened her gaze and held her silent for long moments.

When she finally blinked, he wrenched his gaze from hers and turned to the length of pipe lying loosely in her hand. A long, thin break revealed the source of the leak, but it looked too regular. The pipe was supple and fairly new, not old and brittle.

"It shouldn't have cracked. Let me see that." He held out his hand.

She dropped the pipe in his hand, careful not to touch him again. He glanced up sideways, but her mouth was firmly compressed and her hands, fisted on her thighs.

Her body language screamed denial of whatever the attraction was that zapped between them. He swallowed the lump in his throat and focused on the pipe, running his thumbs along the slit. "This looks like a knife cut, probably serrated. This is no accident. We need to tell your father, maybe—call the police." The lump in his throat became a boulder in his gut.

A sharp-edged chunk of granite that smashed the small burst of optimism of early morning. Damage in the vineyard when he'd just started working there would be dropped at his door. Because Edwards would slap the chief suspect label on him— the bad apple with a grudge, the ex-con. Lark Creek's claim to infamy. Nothing would ever change now he was the ex-con.

Geilis pinned him with a sharp look. "What time did you leave for town?"

There it was. Suspicion. Doubt . . . Accusation.

Heat rose within as his blood and his anger roared his innocence. His impotent rage at the hand fate had dealt him.

"I left as soon as I washed up after we came in from the morning's work. I'd just started eating lunch when you called me. And no, I didn't cut the pipe." He pushed to his feet and strode back to the cellar door. Anger vibrated through him, stamped into the earth with every thud of his boots. Anger, and a ridiculous sense of hurt that Geilis doubted him. He'd worked damned hard to prove himself worthy of Reg Romney's trust. But all it had taken was one look from Geilis, one question and the bars of his prison door clanged shut like thunder. Attitudes to him and his own self-image would ensure he was never free.

"Rick, what's going on?" Reg Romney looked up as Rick pushed the patio door open and stepped into the relative coolness of the cellar.

Dragging in a deep breath, he forced his voice to stay calm, neutral. Always neutral. "We've had some malicious damage. A deliberate cut in the pipe on the lower terrace. Geilis found it before too much damage was done, but we'll have to replace the pipe before we can irrigate everything above that section."

Reg frowned and leaned his good arm on the counter. "That's—odd. Do you think it might have been kids?"

"No reason to think so. It's a long cut. The water gushing must have been intended to damage vines and, at the very least, cause inconvenience."

Geilis appeared behind him, pulled up a stool and sat beside him.

"Gei, you're soaked." Reg pulled a hand towel from under the counter and handed it to her.

She wiped her face and dried her hands. Watching her father's face, she scrunched the towel in her hands. "Rick thinks it was caused by a serrated knife. Shall I call the police?"

Reg shook his head. "I'll do it if you think we need to. But how bad is the damage?"

Geilis huffed out a frustrated sigh. "We've lost some soil and several vines may have been damaged, but it would have been much worse if I hadn't gone back for my secateurs when I did."

Rick pulled the key from his pocket and held it out to Reg. "I found this on the ground near the stopcock. Is it for the shed?"

Reg took the key and examined both it and the pirate tag. Shaking his head he handed the key to Geilis. "I don't recognise it. Do you?"

She looked at the key. "It's a different brand to our vineyard keys. I'll ask the other staff if one of them has lost a key. Where was it again?"

Rick met her gaze. "In a clump of grass near the stopcock. It caught the sun or I wouldn't have noticed it." He turned from Geilis to her father. "Reg, do you have more pipe and connectors or do I need to go into town to buy some?"

Geilis jumped off the stool. "We've got spare lengths. I'll show you and we'll get started on repairs now."

A muscle jumped in Rick's cheek as he followed her out of the cellar door. Knowing how Geilis felt about him, he didn't want to spend time with her. She'd been against her father hiring him in the first place and now . . . the drama of the day would cement her antipathy towards him. Hell, after the day he'd had, he craved solitude and exercise more challenging than working on the vines. He needed a hard twenty-ks pounding the back roads before he'd even begin to forget how loathed his presence in town was.

"That lower section won't need watering for a few days, but the rest of the terraces will." Geilis led the way down the stone steps.

Rick's pace quickened. The less time he had to spend with her, the better. "If you've got a diversion tap I'll put that into the line so we can close off that section while we water the upper terraces." His voice came out gruff, but he managed— just—to say nothing other than about the task ahead.

"Good idea. You're not just a pretty face, are you?" She tossed the comment over her shoulder as she turned the corner and headed for the work shed.

He wished he could see her expression, but Geilis strode ahead of him. She rarely moved without striding, as though to go more slowly was a waste of time. And he knew time was even more precious now. They had to keep the water up to the rest of the vines while they repaired the vandalism. But her comment was the closest she'd come to acknowledging she knew he wasn't the culprit. Not the bad guy. After that awkward interrogation about his movements at lunch, it was a start. But her changing mood disoriented him. One second he was under suspicion, the next he was—*not just a pretty face?*

"So I'm the muscle *and* a pretty face." Uncensored and out of the blue, his thought turned into words. Spoken words that escaped his carefully filtered interactions.

A sound suspiciously like a snort erupted and Geilis came to an abrupt halt. Only the fact his gaze had been riveted on the rhythmic swaying of her bottom stopped him crashing into her. Quickly his focus rose and met her troubled green gaze.

"Look, for what it's worth, I'm sorry if you thought I was questioning you for any reason other than to try to work out when the damage occurred. You were on the lower section last and I only meant to ask—" Her hands gripped one another and she turned away.

He caught her elbow and stopped her before she entered the shed. "Leave it. It's not a problem. And just so you know, Wednesdays are my check in day at the police station."

"Check in? What do you mean? I thought you'd been released from prison for good?"

He realised he still held her arm only when she gently tugged it free. "Early release for good behaviour. I still have to report in every week and keep my nose clean. Any trouble and they can send me back to complete the sentence." With that in mind, Rick decided returning to Vacy's was out of the question, no matter how much he wanted transport of his own. Vacy could so easily claim a disturbance at his premises if he chose to get narky. Revenge for his son's problems might be too tempting.

Geilis tipped her head. "I didn't know that. Guess you'd better avoid the pub on Friday nights then. You don't want to get caught up in a brawl."

He'd add the pub to a growing list of places where he would be *persona non grata.* At this rate, there'd soon be so few places he'd be accepted, let alone welcomed, he'd have to retreat to the hills out of town and become a hermit like Graham Muggeridge. Perhaps his friend had the right idea. Solitude had a lot going for it.

Geilis stepped through the doorway and headed to the far end of the shed. Coils of black pipe hung off heavy-duty

35

brackets. She pointed past them. "There should be a selection of connectors in one of the drawers in that metal cabinet at the end."

Rick pulled a couple of drawers open before he found what he needed. He checked the connector size against the diameter of the pipe and tossed several into a bucket. He added tools, a knife, and the diversion switch before lifting a coil of pipe onto his shoulder. "I'll get started. If you see Brett, can you send him down to give me a hand?"

"Will do."

* * *

Geilis unhooked her secateurs and set about cleaning the mud off. The malicious damage both angered and unnerved her. All the years they'd lived here, this was the first time such a thing had occurred. Why now?

Brett, their part-time field worker popped his head around the door. "Hey, Gei, your dad said to tell you the police are on their way and could you talk to them 'cos you'll know what they need to hear. Why are the police coming? Did Peyton do something?"

A spark of anger at Brett's assumption pulled Geilis out of her musing. "Of course he didn't. He's working on fixing the problem someone else caused." Ugh, she sounded like Janice Lehmann telling off a naughty student.

"Okay, no need to bite my head off. Sheesh, it's a natural conclusion. I'm heading home. I'm done for the day." Brett sounded peeved. Served him right.

"Okay. See you on Friday." Damn it, what was it about Rick that made her put her foot in her mouth all the time? Was it simply who he was and what he'd done—or was it the way her body seemed to develop a mind of its own around him? He wasn't even her type. Any man she *might* be interested in—one day in some far distant future—would not be an ex-con. He would be a hard-working, upstanding pillar of the community, caring and compassionate, and he'd let her get on with the business of the vineyard without distracting her.

He sounded tame, lame, boring.

Rick's not boring. He's not tame either. Dark undercurrents swirled behind Rick's deep brown eyes. Leashed danger that she somehow knew would never be directed against her, no matter how close to the line she trod. But if someone was out to inflict problems on the vineyard . . .

She slipped the secateurs onto her belt and grabbed a spare pair of gloves. No wonder Rick was so closed off. She'd be defensive too if everyone assumed the worst of her like they did with him. Maybe her father was right. Maybe she had come across as judgemental when Rick arrived.

She was judgemental. This was her family's vineyard and their livelihood depended on lots of goodwill and fitting into the community. But Rick was part of this community and her father had seen fit to give him a chance. She could do no less.

Pulling the door closed, she took a moment to look over the rows of vines, and breathe in the earthy smell of life bursting through the grape skins. The winery was her life. Why had someone set out to harm her family's vineyard? Was it some twisted way of sending a message about Rick's presence here?

Determined to give Rick the chance to prove himself as Dad had suggested, she set off down the slope to help him with repairs until the police arrived. Making an effort would start with treating him like other workers. Surely she could manage a bit of light banter while they worked together.

Afternoon sun glistened on droplets of water splattered across green leaves. Rick sat on a dry patch of path beyond the muddy pool, black pipe coiling around his long legs like some

37

huge python he'd wrestled into submission. As she approached, he inserted a connector into one end.

"Brett's gone home for the day. I'll help you until the police arrive."

His hands stilled for a moment on the pipe. Such a small reaction she would have missed it if she hadn't been watching him. Doubting her ability to remain impassive if she'd been in Rick's shoes, she ploughed on. "Dad asked me to talk to them since I discovered the damage, but it might help if you tell them what you found."

"Pass the hole punch and packet of drippers, will you?"

Sorting through the items in the bucket, she found the packet he needed and dropped to her knees beside him. She slit the packet with her utility knife and offered it to him. "Here. Rick, did you hear me?"

He shook out a couple of drippers, and pointed to the length of damaged pipe lying near the fence. "Show them that. It's self explanatory."

"If you don't want to talk to them, just say so."

At last he raised his head and looked at her. "I don't want to talk to them. But Edwards won't accept that. He'll demand to talk to me and you can bet he'll try to lay this at my feet."

Geilis suppressed her gasp before it exploded into a ridiculous denial. Hadn't she already seen how blame played out for Rick? Knowing Sergeant Edwards, it wasn't much of a stretch to imagine the police officer's attitude. But she couldn't help herself. "Don't be silly. Did you see him when you were at the police station?"

"Yeah. I saw him." An unmistakeable chill imbued his terse response.

"Well then, he can't blame you when *he's* your alibi."

"He'll find a way." A half-laugh escaped and some of the tension leached from Rick's expression. "But damn, I'd love to see his face if you tell him he can vouch for me."

Chapter Six

Rick settled quietly into the deep shadows of the trees for the third evening in a row and scanned the unlit buildings of the winery. If Edwards knew he was coming back to the vineyard after hours, he'd have no hesitation about shutting him up in a cell and throwing away the key. But the vandalism worried Rick. He didn't believe in coincidence. Both Reg and Geilis had said nothing like this had happened before and the fact it had happened so soon after Rick began working for the Romney family was cause enough for him to be involved.

A nearly full moon sat high in the sky, bathing the countryside in silvery-grey light. Rick couldn't move out of the shadows without risking discovery, but if the perpetrator returned he would be visible to Rick. Catching the culprit would go a long way to making Rick feel better. If his presence was the reason for the attack, then he was responsible for stopping further damage to the vines.

He waited patiently, grateful for the bushcraft training Graham Muggeridge had given him. So many days when his stepfather had made home unbearable he'd run away into the hills. The hermit hadn't exactly welcomed him at first, but on his second visit, Graham had shown him how to light a fire without matches. The next time he'd taught him how to make a snare and, later, how to track. Over Rick's fraught teenage years, a friendship had grown. It was past time he went looking for Graham again. Maybe on his next free weekend . . .

The lights at the Romney house further up the hill went out soon after nine o'clock. Moon shadows lengthened as the moon began its descent. From the creek magpie-larks called, the two note sound carrying on the still air. A low moo carried across the paddock and soft rustlings in the long grass on the other side of the fence reminded him that nocturnal creatures were on the move.

And then . . . The soft footfall was distinctive amongst the night sounds. Human, not animal, and wearing soft shoes. Heading in his direction.

Silently Rick moved into position as the figure crept closer, keeping to the darker shadows of the tree line along the fence. But Rick's night vision was more than a match for the attempt at stealth. He tracked the progress of the figure as it approached his hiding spot until . . .

Rick sprang forwards tackling the figure to the ground. A loud 'oof' exploded before Rick sat on a slightly built body and grabbed his arms. Slender wrists tried to twist out of his hold. A floral scent that had nothing to do with grapes rose to his nostrils as he turned the intruder over and spread his arms wide. The hood fell back and Geilis bucked her hips trying to throw him off. She fought with all her might and her fingers clawed the air seeking his face.

"Geilis!"

Just her name, but it was all she needed. She lay still and peered up, the ambient light enough to make out her wide eyes. "Rick, what are you doing? Get off me."

"What am I doing here? What the hell do you think you're doing creeping around late at night? I could be anyone."

"You're someone and you're damned well squashing me."

Astride her hips and pinning her to the ground wasn't just squashing her. It was the closest he'd come to a woman in months, and Geilis wasn't just any woman. Something about her stirred a spark. And stirred a nascent physical response she'd feel if he didn't move . . .

Rolling off her, he gripped her hand and elbow and hauled her back into the deepest shadows. "Why are you creeping around like a Ninja all by yourself?"

"Why are you crouching like a snake in the grass?"

"I asked first."

"You pinned me to the ground, so answer me—why are you here?"

He rubbed the back of his neck and scanned the vineyard. "Same reason I'm guessing you're here—to catch a vandal. If he hasn't heard us rolling around on the ground, I reckon we've a chance of nabbing him . . . if he comes calling again. Sit there and don't move. And—"

He reached for the hood of her jacket to cover her hair, but she turned her face at the same moment. Soft lips brushed his hand. Tingles like sparks from a sparkler ran up his skin and he froze. In deep shadow he could see little more than a glint of eyes, a light smudge where her lips parted and revealed her teeth. But he could hear her gasp, feel her soft breath on his wrist. Their encounter was affecting her as much as him.

With fingers that felt less sure of themselves, he touched her cheek. Her face turned into his hand and her breath caught on a barely audible intake. He tipped his head to the left, so focused on Geilis he almost missed the carefully shaded light bobbing towards the cellar door.

The intrusion dragged him away from lust-fuelled images of Geilis and him. "Did you see that?"

Geilis sat up and turned her head to follow his pointing finger. "Someone's trying to break in. Come on. We've got him."

He gripped her arm and drew her close, his mouth close to her ear. "There's no *we*, Geilis. You stay here and call the police. I'll tackle him."

A sharp intake of breath warned him before the muscles in her arm tightened. She fisted her hand and pulled out of his grasp. But she kept her voice low. "This is my vineyard and *you* can call the police if you like. *I'm* going to catch the bastard who dared to vandalise *my* property." She took off at a crouching run.

"Geilis, come back." With no other choice, he ran after her. Anger bubbled up, swift and urgent. They had no idea who they were going to face, no idea if the intruder was armed. Alone. Dangerous.

Damn the woman. Doesn't she have any sense?

Geilis flattened herself against the stone wall, eased the cellar door open and peered around the doorway. Against the pale stone façade they were exposed and visible in the spill of security lighting on the corner of the building. Inside, someone who wished the Romneys harm was on the loose. If there was an accomplice, a lookout man, they were sitting ducks.

He stepped in front of her and leaned down to whisper, "Geilis, for God's sake, leave him to me."

She shook her head and her floral scent wafted into his nostrils. "You can go in first, but I'm coming in right behind you." Shuffling followed by the scrape of metal against metal put a stop to their argument. "What's he doing? If he's touching my wine I'll—"

"Stay behind me." Rick slipped past her and eased through the narrowest opening he could manage. He stood for a moment, allowing his eyes to adjust to the internal darkness before he edged along the wall, feeling his way forward. Geilis touched his arm and he slid his hand down and gripped hers. If he held onto her she couldn't dart past him. If he held onto her she wouldn't try to take on the intruder in some misguided belief that owning the vineyard gave her the right to make the first move.

In the darkness of the cellar the intruder was a shadowy outline behind his torch, which, by its angle, he gripped in his mouth. There was a crack, followed by a splashing sound and Geilis' hand convulsed in his. She leaned around him even as he tried to keep her from seeing what he saw.

"My wine!" The cry tore from Geilis' throat and she lunged into the cellar, dragging him with her.

The torchlight bobbled as the intruder shifted the torch from his mouth to his hand and trained it on Geilis. She threw both hands in front of her face and Rick saw his chance. He pushed her out of harm's way, out of the direct torchlight and raced around the line of casks towards the man. Something flew towards him. He ducked, but cold metal caught him on the temple. He stumbled, slipped in a puddle of wine and fell. His knees crunched against the flagstones. A door banged and the next thing he knew Geilis was at his side and the cellar lights were growing brighter as the LED bulbs warmed.

"Rick, are you okay? Oh my God, you're bleeding." She sank to her knees in front of him and took hold of his chin. "Let me see."

He lifted his head and raised a hand to his throbbing temple. A crowbar lay on the floor beside him, but the intruder was gone. "Damn it, let me go." Pain slammed through his head and one knee as he forced himself to stand. Nausea welled in his gut and he swallowed against the rising tide of bile. Suppressing a groan he took a deep breath and limp-ran through the door.

The night was dark after the bright cellar lights and Rick teetered at the top of a short flight of concrete stairs off the loading dock. Desperately seeking a flicker of movement, the flash of a torch to show him which way to go, he cursed under his breath.

An engine revved, gears crunched and a car burst from a stand of trees, fishtailing onto the gravel driveway that led to the winery. Headlights flicked on a short distance down the road and disappeared over the rise towards town.

A dull metallic thud registered as Geilis smacked the metal railing beside Rick. "Did we lose him?" Regret and anger laced her words.

Bitterness tasted like bile in the back of Rick's throat. Alone, he would have caught the man, but Geilis' outburst at the wrong moment had given the advantage to the intruder. That head start and the blinding torchlight. No use pointing the finger. "Did you get a look at him?"

She turned to look at him and the anger leached from her voice. "No. Didn't you?"

Rick shook his head, immediately regretting the movement. Energy drained from his body and he slumped onto the top step.

"Rick? Are you okay? I'll call an ambulance." She pulled her mobile from her pocket.

Lousy as he was feeling, the last thing he wanted right now was a trip to hospital and several hours sitting in Emergency. He reached over and covered her hand. "Don't. I'll be fine."

"Don't be such a—male. You might have a concussion."

"Geilis, leave it. I've survived worse than this." Squinting against the pain in his head and the spill of light through the doorway, he was worried. She looked pale. Where he had expected violence, Geilis was shocked by what had happened. Her hand shook beneath his.

Abruptly she dropped onto the step below him and hung her head. "If only I hadn't been so stupid."

"What are you talking about?" He leaned his head against the cool bricks and tried to concentrate on what she was saying.

"Calling out like I did. If I hadn't warned him, you might have caught him. He could have been tied up and waiting for the police to take him away. And you wouldn't have been hurt." Her shoulders hunched and without thinking, he raised a hand. To touch her? Pat her shoulder—pull her close? But the yellowish security lighting revealed his bloodied hand in gory detail. Pulling back, he felt the stickiness of his blood in the crease lines of his hand, tasted the iron taint as his tongue touched his lips. The smell of blood didn't sicken him. But he wouldn't allow it to touch Geilis.

She wiped a hand across her cheeks and stood, staring off into the empty darkness. How long she stayed like that he didn't know. His eyelids closed and he drifted on a sea of pain. Eventually he heard a decisive sniff. "Okay, no ambulance, but come inside and let me clean the blood off and check your wound."

Rick didn't want to think about how close they'd come to catching the man. He didn't want to move. He wanted to sleep and . . .

Geilis shook his shoulder. "Rick—"

The note of panic roused him and he realised his eyes were shut. A sharp pain stabbed when he turned his head and opened his eyes and he quickly closed them again.

"Talk to me now or I'm calling the ambulance."

He covered her hand with his clean one where she clutched his shoulder. Her pulse was racing—with fear for him? "Don't. I'll get up." The rough-dressed brick scraped his right arm as he pushed upright and his head spun like he'd just come off a Gravitron ride. Geilis picked up his left arm and set it across her shoulders. Slowly they made their way to the kitchen, each step jarring no matter how carefully he stepped. Pain shot through his knee—head—knee—head—

She guided him onto a chair and he leaned his head against the wall and closed his eyes. As though from a distance he heard the scrape of metal, the squeak as Geilis opened the medical kit. Quick footsteps imparted a sense of urgency as Geilis moved around the kitchen.

Cold water dripped onto his arm and her voice roused him. "This may sting a bit." He hissed as the cold cotton wipe touched his wound, but didn't open his eyes.

***

"Rick, don't you dare go to sleep." Geilis watched the flicker of his eyelids, the movement of his eyeballs beneath the thin skin. He sat still. Sluggish and pale, so unlike the leashed strength Rick exuded. She bit her lip and kept her focus on cleaning off the blood. So much blood.

My fault.

Her mind raced as she sifted through details from her first aid course of how to treat head injuries, but guilt distracted her. What was a cask of wine compared to Rick's injury? Her fingers trembled as she dabbed at the last stubborn patch of blood around his wound. Cleaned, it didn't look big enough to have bled so much, but the area around it had begun to darken and swell. At least the blood had stopped oozing, but she covered the site with a sterile pad.

"Rick, can you hear me?" She took hold of his hand and felt for his pulse. Strong and steady. "Rick, squeeze my hand if you can hear me."

His fingers wrapped around hers and she could have sobbed with relief. But now what? He couldn't drive home in his condition and he'd made it clear he didn't want her to call for help. Her gaze fell on the door to the office. Her father had made up a camp bed in there for nights when he worked late. If it was still in there . . .

"Don't move. I'll be back in a minute." Backing away, she kept her eyes on Rick until the corner cabinet jabbed her bottom. Quickly, she entered the office and flicked the light on. The bed was folded against the back wall. Thank goodness her father hadn't got around to taking it back up to the house before his heart attack. She set the bed up and tossed a pillow onto one end and then scooted back out to Rick.

Bruising and an egg-sized bump on his temple brought her guilt roaring back. "Rick, wake up. You need to lie down. I've made up a bed for you. Rick?" Anxiously she shook his shoulder and leaned closer. His breathing was regular, but maybe she should have phoned for an ambulance. Maybe she would just . . .

"Still don't need one." His words were a little slurred, but his eyes were cracked open just enough to reassure her.

"How did you know what I was thinking?"

"Your thumb is hovering above your phone." With a visible effort he pushed to his feet and gripped the edge of the cupboard. He swayed like a giant oak tree. "You mentioned bed?"

"In the office. Come with me." Without asking, she slipped his arm over her shoulders again. If he collapsed she doubted she'd be able to get him back on his feet. He was heavier than she remembered. Or perhaps she only noticed it now the adrenaline had gone. It was only ten metres from kitchen to camp bed, but she felt as though she'd carried him miles through clinging mud. Worry sat, adding to the weight of his arm on her shoulders.

They staggered around the desk and Rick half-fell onto the bed. He managed to raise one leg before he covered his eyes with an arm. The other leg hung over the side. Geilis lifted it onto the bed and drew a light blanket over him and then sat, watching the rise and fall of his chest.

Too worried to leave him alone, she made a cup of black coffee and settled beside the camp bed. Dawn was four hours away and she needed to know he was going to be okay.

Chapter Seven

Rick woke with a thumping headache and a sick feeling he was back in the narrow bed in his prison cell. His feet hung over the end of the thin mattress and he felt as though he'd roll onto the floor if he turned over. And there was an unfamiliar weight across his chest. It was warm and heavy and a faint hint of flowers teased his nostrils. Tentatively he raised his left hand and felt the shape of a head, thick hair, a plait. His fingers explored the length of that plait as memory filtered back. He opened his eyes and then slitted them against the early morning sun streaming through the window.

Geilis sprawled across him, her face turned towards his and her head resting on her arm. It curved up and her hand rested against his ear lobe so softly her touch tickled. "Gei—"

Dry-throated, he had to swallow and try again. His voice came out rough and raspy. "Geilis?"

She wriggled a little as though making herself more comfortable, but didn't wake. Had she watched over him through the night?

The thought of her keeping watch while he slept disturbed him. Certain the crimes targeting the winery weren't random, that they were somehow linked to his arrival at the vineyard, Geilis' involvement on any level created a conflict in him. People didn't do things for him; he did things to help others. Being on the receiving end felt—odd.

A sigh, and the light puff of her breath across his cheek cut off his meandering thoughts.

In this moment—a moment stolen from time, unlikely to occur again—he could forget how people regarded him. How

Geilis eyed him with suspicion. Geilis awake was prickly, decisive, with a hard edge that kept most people at a distance. Especially him. And yet he admired her single-minded dedication to her work. Not that she'd appreciate hearing that from him.

But in this moment he was simply the man she'd looked after, the man who was grateful to her. He revelled in the softness of her hair and the warmth of her body sprawled across his. It felt normal, like life should be; like it might have been if he hadn't made the choice to protect Harvey.

She stirred, shifted on his chest, and went still. Too still.

"Rick?" Her eyes opened, blinked. Abruptly she sat up and one hand rose to push her hair out of her eyes. "Gosh, I'm sorry. Did I fall asleep on you?"

"Maybe. It's fine." Gingerly he eased up onto his elbow. "How's your head feel?"

"Like a blacksmith's anvil." He licked dry lips.

Geilis jumped to her feet. "I'll get you some water and put the kettle on. Back in a minute." She pulled the door open and her hand flew up to her mouth.

Reg stood in the doorway, mobile phone in hand and thumb hovering over the green button. He looked from Geilis to Rick and back to his daughter. "We've had a break in. I was about to call the police. What the devil's going on here?"

"Dad, I—we—we almost caught an intruder last night."

"What do you mean *last night*? You knew and didn't think to tell me?"

"Rick got hurt and we lost the man."

"And again—why didn't you wake me?"

Rick swung his legs over the edge of the camp bed and stood slowly, one hand on the desk helping him keep his balance. "Geilis was worried I had a concussion. I was pretty much out of it for a while. I'm sorry we didn't manage to catch whoever it was."

Reg's mouth opened and closed without a word slipping out until his gaze settled on his daughter. "Come into the kitchen. We'll put the kettle on and then you can both tell me what happened. Let's start with what you were doing at the vineyard after hours."

Rick kept it brief, omitting the fact he'd tackled Geilis to the ground. Her father didn't need to know and he was certain she'd be embarrassed at having been caught out. "He threw the crowbar and I was slow getting out of its way. I'm sorry, Reg. We were so close to nabbing him." He picked up the steaming mug of coffee Geilis set in front of him and sipped.

Geilis sat next to her father and wrapped both hands around her mug. "What Rick didn't mention was that if I hadn't yelled out when I realised the man was smashing my—our—wine, then we would probably have caught him. It's my fault he got away."

"I don't care so much that he escaped, but Geilis, you put yourself in danger. We'll call the police and this time I'll be very clear with them. Tony Edwards had better damned well get off his backside and catch this bloke before he strikes again. Rick, son, you look like shit. Take the day off."

"I'm sure I'll be f—"

"That's an order. Get some rest. And you, missy—" Reg shook his head. "We'd best think what we'll say to your mother. She'll have conniptions if she finds out you were facing off with an intruder, with or without Rick by your side. Now, how about you drive Rick home, make sure he gets inside safely, and get your story straight before you talk to your mother. In the meantime, I'll call the police. Again."

"Sure, Dad. Back in a little while."

Rick followed Geilis out to the winery van and climbed into the passenger seat. Every bump in the road felt like jackhammers starting up and his head weighed a ton. He leaned against the window when Geilis stopped at a stop sign, but the vibrations of the car made his teeth rattle. The drive back to Thornyhill Farm was accomplished in silence and a prayer for unconsciousness until Geilis pulled up next to the front steps.

Breathing a sigh of relief, Rick opened his door and stepped out before meeting her gaze. Swelling around the wound was forcing his left eye to close and he couldn't wait for the right eye to join the party in sleep. "Thanks for the ride."

"Before you go . . ."

His gut heaved as though he was on a small boat in choppy seas. Unsure and frankly not caring what Geilis was going to say, he clung to the doorframe and prayed he'd make it inside before he was sick. "What?"

"Thanks for doing what you did. For trying to keep an eye out for us. I'm sure you're wrong though. I'm sure these—incidents—have nothing to do with you. I don't think it would be a wise move to share that idea with the police." Her face was a pale blur, but there was a sharp edge to her words that registered even through his pain.

"You're probably right." He wouldn't mention his suspicion to Edwards. But he wasn't prepared to give up his growing certainty that he was the reason the vineyard had been targeted.

There's no such thing as coincidence. Graham Muggeridge had taught him that, and, regardless of how others treated the hermit on his rare appearances in town, Rick respected his friend's intelligence and native cunning.

He shut the door and leaned down to speak through the open window. Geilis' mouth tipped up in a quick smile—at least he thought it was a flash of white teeth—but it disappeared and a frown took its place. Shadows under her eyes told their own story of the night they'd shared. If only he'd ducked faster. If only he'd caught the intruder; then, tired as she was, that worry would have been negated.

"I'll be back in the morning." He turned and climbed the stairs to Travis' front door and headed for the comfort of his bed.

Funny thing, he thought as his eyes closed; confined as it was, he'd felt more comfortable in that narrow camp cot with Geilis' head on his chest than he'd felt since before his arrest. Comfort was a relative term. Comfort was a woman like Geilis by his side.

He wouldn't know that sort of comfort again.

Chapter Eight

What was wrong with her? Geilis' focus was shot to pieces and her second coffee of the morning was rapidly cooling as she sat in the armchair under the window, only half listening to her father talking to Sergeant Edwards. Her father's explanation of last night's events sounded more like an adventure than the night of high drama she and Rick had endured. Constable Brooks sat on Geilis' left quietly taking notes. The policewoman caught her eye and gave a little smile.

Dad ended his evidence with, "We can't thank Rick enough for his help, but it's a pity he was injured protecting our property."

Edwards' expression was sour. Did he really dislike Rick so much he couldn't give credit where credit was due? The sergeant looked from her father to her. "I want his testimony. Why didn't you keep him here instead of letting him run off home?"

Geilis had had enough of the police officer's arrogance. "Rick was concussed last night. He needed rest so I drove him home. Surely you can interview him tomorrow? I doubt our burglar will be back tonight."

"I wouldn't count on it."

"What do you mean? Rick frightened him off." The insinuation in Edwards' bald statement caught her off guard and her heart skipped a beat before speeding up. Vague menace had lurked behind the torch, a menace that had injured Rick and had her questioning her sanity. How could she have thought she could take on an intruder without help? If Rick hadn't returned to the vineyard, hadn't insisted he led the way into the cellar, it might have been her with a concussion. Or worse. A shiver crept down her spine and she swallowed against the bile threatening to erupt from her throat.

"Maybe. But have you considered your new hired hand might be in on this? He could be casing your business and planning to rob you with outside help." Edwards nodded as though the idea weren't totally outrageous, as though he could *see* his version unfolding before his eyes.

Geilis snorted. "Do you seriously think he'd arrange to be knocked on the head to make it look like he wasn't involved? That's ridiculous."

"Miss Romney, you're conveniently forgetting this man is a criminal. He's been released early, supposedly for *good behaviour.*" He spat out the last two words as though they left a bad taste in his mouth.

"That sounds like you don't believe in second chances, sergeant?" Oh how she disliked the police officer. Would he do anything to find their intruder or had he already decided Rick was his man?

"Once a crim, always a crim. Comes from bad blood. Don't let him hoodwink you into thinking he's decent. He's not."

Out of the corner of her eye, her father made eye contact with her and gave a small shake of his head. He turned back to Edwards and stood, hand extended and ready to see the police officer to the door. "I hope you find out who's trying to upset things here, Tony, but I for one am prepared to take Rick as I find him, and so far, he's done nothing to shake my faith in him."

Angry red coloured Edwards' face, but he rose and shook her father's hand. "Don't say I didn't warn you. Brooks, let's go." He ignored Geilis and lumbered through the door and down the hall.

Constable Brooks closed her notebook and looked at Geilis. "That was very brave of you, but please don't take on any more burglars on your own. Lock yourself in a safe room and call us if there is a next time." She smiled to take any sting out of her words.

"You can count on it."

Marion Brooks nodded, added, "Good to hear," and followed her superior out of the room.

Geilis slumped in her chair. Her eyes felt like they were hanging out on stalks. That's what her *bravery* had done for her. She picked up the mug of coffee, drank a mouthful and grimaced. It was stone cold and unpalatable. She set it down on the coaster as her father returned and sat in the armchair opposite.

"Seems like Rick has an enemy in Tony."

Geilis' head fell back against the squishy padding of the armchair and energy drained from her body now the police had left. "Just because Rick committed some offence? That's crazy."

"I think Tony's taking out his dislike of Rick's stepdad, Garrett, on Rick."

"Why would he do that?" Stifling a yawn, Geilis curled her legs up and rested her head on her hand.

"Aside from the fact Garrett Thomas is a nasty piece of work and has been in jail as often as not? Garrett got the better of Tony one night down at the pub. Gave him a bloody nose and set Tony on his backside in the middle of an attempted arrest." Her father chuckled. The sight must have been amusing because her father didn't generally laugh at others' misfortunes. "Tony's not the sort to forgive injury to his dignity. When Rick got arrested Tony seemed to take it as corroboration Rick was following in Garrett's footsteps."

"But Rick isn't his stepfather. He's nothing like Garrett Thomas. Besides, was Rick even in the pub that night?"

"I don't recall, but likely not. He couldn't stand being in the same house as Garrett; once Rick turned eighteen, he spent more time away than at home, especially after his mother passed away. If Garrett was drinking in the pub, Rick would have turned around and walked out." Her father pinched his bottom lip and looked at her over the top of his glasses. "I know you were—reluctant when Rick came to work here, but how do you feel now?"

Her insides cringed at the memory of her reaction to Rick's arrival and her father's words that first morning. Rick still unsettled her, but not for the reason her father imagined. "He's a good worker; anyone can see that."

"But . . .?"

But?

Working with him created a whole new problem. Rick was distraction with a capital D. A distraction that came with a wholly unsuitable desire to do something about it, if she were honest.

But . . .

Anything and anyone who took her focus from her work should go, but her father was right; they needed Rick's muscle. Last night's encounter had rattled her more than she would admit and she craved the sense of security his presence gave her.

"I trust him." There, she'd said it and it was true. She trusted him to work hard and do what was right. In the vineyard. As for how he made her feel, nobody was going to know that Rick's presence distracted her to the extent that she'd cut a small bunch of grapes because she'd been watching him walk past. "You trust him and Merle Leonard thought the world of him and both of you are excellent judges of character. I think we'll just have to be extra vigilant until the vandals are caught."

"That's good then. If you weren't sure about him, much as I wouldn't want to, I'd have let him go."

"Really? That wouldn't be fair on Rick, Dad." She managed to keep her response low-key, but she was taken aback by her father's comment. Growing up, he'd been the one to help her see things from a different perspective. To walk in someone else's shoes, he'd called it. That was how she'd first connected with Katy on the bank of the creek, back when they were ten years old. Katy's loneliness and need for a friend had been apparent to Geilis once her father pointed out he'd never seen her with a little friend her own age. "Rick doesn't deserve to be shunted aside when he's trying so hard."

"You're my first priority, Gei. You and your mother. But I'm pleased you're reconciled to working with Rick now. He can do the hard yakka for you until I'm better. And maybe—"

"Maybe what?"

Her father shook his head and drew her to her feet. "Maybe it's time we had lunch and gave your mother a potted version of last night's events. She'll have seen the police car and be champing at the bit to know why. Come on."

***

Rick woke to a sky streaked with pink, purple and gold. And a tender spot that hurt when he turned and the egg-sized bump on his head touched the pillow. He sucked in a breath, blinked as the pain subsided, and then checked the time on his phone. Last night, before his abortive trip to the vineyard, he'd offered to cook dinner tonight. Travis would soon be home, and hungry.

59

SUSANNE BELLAMY

With a groan Rick swung his legs over the side of his bed and stood. The musty smell of slept-in clothes wafted around him, a fume of blood, dirt and sweat. He stripped off and dropped his blood-streaked clothes into the washing basket and lurched into the bathroom for a quick shower.

Revived and clean, but with a dull headache and a partially closed left eye, he pulled on clean clothes and set about preparing a simple meal of steak and vegetables. He'd just finished peeling the potatoes when Travis drove past the kitchen window on the quad bike.

A minute later he came through the back door and went straight to the fridge. "Beer?"

Rick turned and shook his head. "Not for me. Dinner won't be long."

"Christ, mate, what happened to you?" Travis stared, shock evident in his expression.

"I don't look that bad, do I?" He reached up and gingerly touched his swollen eye.

"Mate, you'd frighten the kids worse than me and that's saying something." Travis' scarred cheek had been the reason he'd hidden away at Thornyhill Farm until Katy Leonard had coaxed him back to the land of the living. Rick had joshed him about his pretensions of playing the fairy-tale Beast to Katy's Beauty.

"Let me finish cooking and I'll tell you over dinner." He turned back to the pan and set two steaks to fry. How much of last night's events should he share with Travis? Definitely not the part where he'd woken up with Geilis' head on his chest. That wasn't for anyone else to know. Nor how he'd tackled her to the ground. But could his friend offer some perspective on Rick's theory or was the fact the damage began after his arrival really no more than coincidence?

60

He turned the steaks and began dishing out the vegetables. "Grab the knives and forks, mate. I'm about to serve dinner."

Chapter Nine

Reg had called a meeting before work began for the day and the tasting room was filled with golden light as the small group of outdoor staff settled at round, metal cafe tables and turned their chairs to face Reg.

"It doesn't fit over the egg on my head." Rick dropped his Akubra onto the table and slumped into a chair across from Geilis. Morning light slanted through the French door beside him, the splash of sun already hot on his jeans-clad legs.

"Can I get away with telling you you're big-headed, just this once?" Geilis gave him a grin that was cheeky without hitting flirty. As if Geilis would flirt with him.

It had been a long time since anyone had teased him like that, and it felt nice. "Just this once. Is your dad going to talk about the break in?"

Her smile faded and shadows dimmed her green eyes. He kicked himself for breaking the moment and reminding her of their close call. "I guess so, and other security issues. That really is one heck of a bump you've got. It looks worse now than before. Maybe you should have more time—"

He gritted his teeth. Travis had said much the same thing over breakfast. "I'm fine. I've got a hard head. Nothing's broken."

"Okay, don't grump at me. Actually your skin is broken, but whatever. If you feel up to working, far be it for me to stop you." She turned sideways on her chair, ignoring him and looking at her father who was sorting through his notes.

Damn, Rick didn't mean to grump. He didn't intend to snap at Geilis or break their light-hearted connection. What was the matter with him that he couldn't banter right along with her? Spending most of the past couple of weeks working beside her at tasks Reg would usually have done, Rick should have been better at talking to her by now. He set his elbow on the table and rested his head on his hand. He felt lop-sided and heavy-headed and out of sorts with himself as he stared through the glass-panelled doors.

The vines were loaded with grapes and work in the vineyard was slowly catching up to where Reg said they should be by this time in the season. Reg's heart scare and broken arm had put them behind and Rick would be damned if he'd slack off because of a little bump on his head. He owed Reg big-time for giving him a chance.

Reg called for everyone's attention. Brett, who was often last to arrive, slipped into a chair and sat, eyes glued on his mobile phone hidden behind his hat in his lap as Reg started speaking.

"You've probably all heard by now that we've had a couple of incidents. A pipe was deliberately cut in the vineyard, and a cask was smashed in the cellar. The intruder was disturbed before he got a chance to do too much damage. We lost one cask of chardonnay, but our losses could have been much worse. Lark Creek isn't like the city; most of us haven't been in the habit of locking our homes or vehicles. Security has been lax up to this point. That changes from now on."

Rick's attention zoned in and out, but he got the gist of Reg's new security measures and approved of everything. Except that Geilis was given the task of locking up at the end of each day. No matter how independent she was, he didn't like the fact she'd be alone as she made the final round before dark.

As the staff filtered away to their daily jobs, he hung back intending to have a word with Reg, but his employer beat him to it. "Rick, don't go. I want a word with you." He turned back to finish his conversation with Brett who looked less than pleased before he, too, went back to work.

Reg picked up his notes and came over to join Rick at the table. "I've got a proposition I want to run by you."

Geilis had risen from her chair, but she stopped in her tracks, a frown furrowing her brow as she put a hand on her father's shoulder. "Is this something I need to know about?"

Reg reached up and awkwardly patted her hand. "Probably. I'm going to ask Rick to do something for me—for us and I'm not sure if you'll like it, but after the other night . . ."

Rick nodded and clasped his hands loosely between his knees. "Maybe it's the same as what I was going to suggest, Reg. Until whoever's targeting the winery is caught, I'd like to lock up at the end of the day—"

"Not on your Nelly." Geilis cut him off at the knees. Where her winery was concerned, nobody was going to take over any of her tasks without a fight.

Rick raised both hands in surrender. "That didn't come out right. I meant *with* Geilis. To accompany her so she's not alone."

"I don't need you to hold my hand while I turn a key or two."

Reg shook his head. "Kind of you, Rick, and I think it's a sensible idea having two sets of eyes checking everything. Thanks. I wish I'd thought of it."

"But Dad—"

"Gei, this isn't negotiable." His gaze flicked up to Rick's wound and his mouth pinched. His daughter might have been the one confronting the burglar alone if Rick hadn't taken matters into his own hands and kept watch. Rick's gut flipped at the thought of Geilis putting herself in such danger again. Whatever Reg suggested he'd agree to, so long as it kept Geilis safe. "But I'm happy to discuss my other idea with you."

"Do you mean there's something else you think I won't agree with?"

"Maybe." He held her gaze and his shoulders went back as he sat tall in his seat. He wore a look of determination and Rick got a sense of what the young Reg had been like, the man with a dream who had created a winery from scratch on an old sheep farm thirty years ago. Geilis might not like what was coming, but Rick was pretty sure her father would get his way this time, the offer of discussion notwithstanding.

"Rick, I'd like to offer you an additional job. Besides providing what Geilis calls *the muscle*, I'd like you to keep an eye on the place at night. Kind of like a security guard. Comes with room and board. D'you need time to think about it?"

"No, sir. I accept." It would make accompanying Geilis at the end of the day a natural part of his job. And if he was living here, his chances of catching the intruder were greatly increased.

"Do I get any say in this, Dad?" Was it anger or annoyance that turned Geilis' cheeks red? Or had the idea already occurred to her how absurd it was to hire an ex-con to keep their vineyard safe?

"Of course, but I thought you said you didn't have a problem when we spoke the day Rick started work here. Did I misunderstand?" Reg pinned Geilis with a look that challenged his daughter to disagree.

She met his gaze. Eventually, she sat back and shoved her hands into her jeans pockets. "No problem. It's a sensible idea. Where are you thinking of putting him?"

"In the old shearers' shed. Rick, Gei can show you where to go. Check it out and then come up to the house and Jill will give you bedding for your bunk."

"Sure." Automatically Rick reached for his hat.

"Big head, remember." Geilis smirked, but there was a troubled look in her eyes. She didn't want him staying here; that much was clear. It was the *why* that bothered Rick. Security required a high degree of trust in an employee. If she felt so strongly about him being an ex-con, how could she trust him in the new role Reg had cast him in? She strode to the door, calling over her shoulder, "Come on, Mr Potato-head."

Fiddling with his Akubra, Rick turned to Reg and held out his hand. "Thanks, Reg. I appreciate your trust. I won't let you down."

"I know that, son. Don't let Gei's little outburst trouble you. She's in a tricky spot—making some decisions for the winery without having complete control because I'm still here. We're treading a fine line, her and me, and you got caught in her uncertainty."

"Not a problem." He understood the uncertainty of no man's land. He lived in it every day.

***

Geilis started the engine of the quad bike and stared straight ahead. "Hop on. We'll pick up the bedding on the way over." Hiring Rick as extra security was a good idea. The thought of her darling father coming face to face with another intruder appalled her. Rick would cope. Rick would have caught the man last time if not for her. But knowing Rick would be around twenty-four-seven would do nothing else for her peace of mind. Not until she learned to control her imagination around him. She revved the engine as Rick climbed on behind her and took off like a cut snake towards the house.

He grabbed her hips and his long legs bracketed hers, wrapping her in a blanket of heat. "Give a bloke a chance to get settled, why don't you?"

Choosing the quad, which was parked outside, over the ute up in the shed had been a no-brainer. The bike was close and she'd be over and done with Rick that much faster.

Duh. Closer. Why hadn't she factored that into her calculations?

It was almost, but not quite like the full body blanket when he'd tackled her. God, it was as though her subconscious was making bad decisions to push her into his arms. She increased speed and pulled up in front of the house with a slide along the dry grass and waited for Rick to dismount.

He stood aside as she climbed off and followed her to the front veranda. "I'll wait here, unless you need a hand?"

"With carrying a couple of sheets and a towel? As if."

But her mother had other ideas. "Dad rang and let me know the new arrangements. I must say I'm relieved after the trouble you had the other night. Here, I've sorted out a few things to make Rick comfortable."

A few things turned out to be more than the sheets and towel Geilis had envisaged. "Mum, he won't need three pillows, and seriously—a doona in summer?"

"Oh, I forgot the mosquito net. Hang on, darling." Her mother hustled Geilis to the linen cupboard and climbed onto a stool. "Take this, will you. And tell that young man to come up to the house around seven for dinner."

"He's eating with us too?" A sudden desire to make herself scarce instead of sitting across from Rick at dinner tempted her to escape to Katy's for the night. But that would mean giving over control to Rick for the security of her business.

Mum gave her an odd look. "Of course he is. Accommodation and board, Dad told me."

Could the day, week, month get more difficult?

Staggering through the door beneath a mountain of bed linen, the mosquito net balanced precariously on top of the two pillows she'd convinced her mother would do, her antsy attitude dissolved when Geilis spotted Rick lying back on the settler's chair, eyes closed and his chest rising and falling in the pattern of sleep. Beneath his olive skin, his cheeks were pale, a stark contrast to the heavy bruising around his eye.

Her fingers itched to trace the line of his jaw. Thank goodness her hands were full or her silly fascination with Rick might have led her to reveal a weakness where he was concerned. Beside her the screen door slipped from her foot and banged shut. Rick's eyes flew open and his gaze connected with hers.

"Sorry. Did I doze off?" He stood and rolled his head back and around before holding out his hands. "Here, I'll take those."

"Just grab the pillows and the net. I've got the rest."

Her mother scurried onto the veranda waving a giant black garbage bag. "Here, put the bedding into the bag for the trip across the paddock. Stop it from getting dusty."

Rick took the bag with a thank you, and stuffed the pillows inside before holding the bag wide. "Drop your bundle in." He pulled the yellow ties and secured the neck then settled the bag on the rear tray of the bike.

Geilis climbed onto the front while her mother smiled and waved at Rick. "See you for dinner, Rick. Seven not too early for you?"

Both her parents were so accepting of him. Why couldn't she be the same? Accept him as just another employee and get on with running the vineyard.

"Seven is fine. Thank you."

As they bounced over the paddock towards the shearers' shed, an odd feeling took root in Geilis' mind. Things were changing no matter what she did. So if she couldn't stop change, it was up to her to make the best of it. Rick was here for a limited time.

Treat him like you treat other employees.

She pulled up in front of the low set building, a relic of the earlier sheep farm that had occupied the land before her parents turned it into a winery, and jumped off the bike. Rick picked up the bag of bedding and she opened the door into the room on the eastern end. "I think this will be better than the western end. Not so hot in the afternoon."

***

Rick tossed the bag onto the nearest bunk. There were six in total, none of them designed for a man over six feet tall. Not that he was complaining. For the first time in months he had a living space that was entirely his. "This will do me. Thanks."

"I'll help you make the bed." She picked up the bag and began untying the tabs.

He leaned against the upright, folded his arms and watched as she pulled the slipknot undone. "You think I can't make a bed? As if."

Geilis' eyes narrowed as he turned her words back on her. "Fine. Do it yourself." She thrust the bag at his chest and strode to the sink in the corner. With jerky movements she turned the tap on. Pipes clanged and brownish water wheezed from the spout. "This doesn't look nice."

"Leave it run for a bit. It will probably come good once the pipes have cleared. What's the water source?"

"There's a rainwater tank behind the quarters and an outdoor shower underneath the tank. Cold, but that shouldn't be a problem." She flicked the light switches on and off. The interior lights did little against the wash of morning light coming through the windows. "Might be worth checking if the outside lights work too. And see if there's gas in the single burner. It's been ages since anyone has stayed here on a regular basis."

"Geilis, stop worrying. This is luxury compared to camping out in the bush. I'll be fine."

"Okay. If you don't need anything else we should get back to work."

Her manner had whiplashed from annoyed with him to being all about business. While he missed the earlier banter, it was easier this way. If they focused only on business matters, he wouldn't start imagining an impossible relationship. "I'll get set up here, check everything is working and then walk across and join you. I need to phone and let Trav know plans have changed and he's got his spare room back."

"If you're sure . . ."

"I'm sure."

She hesitated, her weight shifting from one foot to the other in a totally un-Geilis-like manner. He'd been on the receiving end of her bluntness enough times to know Geilis like this was not normal. It intrigued him.

"Spit it out. What's wrong?"

Eyes wide, she looked up and pinned him with a direct look. "My parents trust you. Don't do the wrong thing by them or you'll have me to contend with."

Anger flared deep inside and his headache took on a life of its own. What more could he do to convince her he was honest? "That sounds like Sergeant Edwards. Been warning you off hiring me, has he?"

Pink flared in her cheeks confirming his suspicion, but she held his gaze. "Actions speak louder than words. I make up my own mind."

"Do you? So, do you trust me or just tolerate me for your father's sake?" It didn't matter what anyone else thought. He was here and working for Reg because Reg was a decent man who believed in second chances. But Rick's chest felt tight. He wanted Gei to trust him, to like him. Even knowing how crazy it was, he wanted it.

She took a deep breath and let it out slowly before she answered. "In spite of Sergeant Edwards' advice and your recent past, I take people how I find them. I trust you. But that doesn't mean I have to like having you living here." She spun on her heel and strode through the doorway.

Rick sat on the bunk. He'd asked and Geilis had answered. She didn't like him. Any attraction he'd thought was sparking between them was all in his imagination. No matter. Dislike he could manage. He was used to it.

But *trust*? Winning Geilis' trust should have been a high point. Instead, bittersweet, it sat beside her antipathy and mocked him. He couldn't do anything about it except stay out of her way as much as possible. But tonight, at lock up, she'd just have to grin and bear his company because he had a job to do, regardless of how she felt.

Having made up his mind to avoid her as much as possible, he made the bed, checked the water, gas, and lights and made a note of minor repairs that needed to be done before walking back to the workshop.

Summer heat was building and his hat perched uncomfortably on the back of his injured head, ready to topple off at the whiff of a breeze. The workshop was empty at this time of morning, but voices drifted up from the terraces. He assembled a bucket of tools and was about to head down and join the others when the door opened and closed with the soft, furtive sound of someone trying to slip into the shed unseen. Quietly he set the bucket on the floor. Muscles tensed, he waited.

He stepped behind the angle of the wall next to the long bench, and peered around the corner, only mildly surprised when Brett wandered along the far side of the work island. The part-timer hauled himself onto the bench top and lit a cigarette right under the 'No Smoking' sign. He dragged in a lungful of smoke and held it in his mouth as he opened his phone.

Rick stepped out from his hiding place, bucket in hand. "Is it morning tea break all ready?"

Brett gasped, coughed and slid off the bench, expelling a cloud of cigarette smoke. He flapped his hand futilely to disperse the evidence. "What the hell are you doing, man, sneaking up on me like that?"

Rick shrugged. "Looks to me like you're the one doing the sneaking."

"I could ask you the same thing. Everyone else is outside." Brett's expression clouded and his shoulders hunched, spreading his hi-vis shirt like a puffer fish, all air and no substance.

Rick had seen his like in jail. He held up his bucket. "I'm moving from one job to the next. I suggest you do the same."

"Yeah, well I'm expecting an important phone call. Piss off or I'll tell the boss you were slacking. Do you think he'll listen to you—a crim?"

Rick's hand tightened around the bucket handle. He'd shrugged off his share of taunts as a kid, and from more skilful manipulators in jail. Brett's petty niggling was kindergarten level. But here, in Reg's workshop, darkness welled in Rick, and regret for that other life he'd given up when he accepted punishment for his brother's crime. Ex-cons seldom get a break, he reminded himself.

He held Brett's gaze until the other man's slid away. Not by so much as the twitch of a muscle would he give Brett the satisfaction of knowing his words hit their target. He'd redirect the energy required to give Brett a black eye into his work. No way was he blowing the chance Reg had given him.

Brett shifted from foot to foot, and took a quick couple of puffs of his cigarette. Rick recognised the shuffle dance from prison, the weaker man testing his courage to challenge another and settling for an amateurish snide remark when discretion won out.

"Guess I'll wait for my call somewhere the air is fresher."

"You do that." Rick waited until Brett left before slamming a fist down on the bench top. As the darkness inside him descended, a voice ghosted through his memory. His mother's, the first time he'd got into a fight at school.

Never mind what the others call you, darling. You're better, stronger in mind than them. Always remember that. Breathe, and walk away.

He sucked in a deep breath, pushed back the darkness and walked out into the bright morning.

Chapter Ten

"Geilis, dinner's ready, and Rick's here." Her mother's face appeared around the edge of her door. "Are you okay, darling? You look peaky."

"Just tired. I'll be right out to give you a hand, Mum." She'd lingered over her bath and fluffed around in nervous anticipation of Rick joining them instead of helping her mother in the kitchen as she usually did.

"Everything's done. Rick helped me carry the food out to the table. All that's missing is you."

"Sorry." Geilis stood and ran her hands down her sleeveless top. She'd dithered over what to wear and when her mother's glance landed on the pile of discarded clothes on her bed, she squirmed with embarrassment. "Don't look at me like that. It's not what you think."

"What do you think I think, darling? That you like Rick?"

"I don't."

"Clearly." Her mother's smile was gentle, but Geilis had the feeling she was as transparent as glass. "Oh, Mum . . ."

"You look gorgeous. Now get yourself to the table before the roast gets cold. It's pork—your favourite." With a wink, her mother disappeared and moments later, Geilis heard her asking for a glass of wine.

Straightening her shoulders, she flicked her plait over her shoulder and strode down the hallway. As she stepped into the room Rick was handing a glass of wine to her mother. He met her gaze, but his slow smile—the smile that in her mind promised all sorts of delicious distractions—was missing.

"Good evening, Geilis. Would you like a wine?"

Her father sat in his armchair, glass of water in hand. "Rick insisted on doing the honours."

Her mother looked at their guest, a secretive smile tipping up the corners of her mouth. Of course her mother thought Rick had caught her daughter's eye. That damned pile of clothes strewn across her bed was like a neon sign pointing to her weakness for his dark good looks. She pressed her lips together and dug her hands into the pockets of her jeans. Rocking back on her heels, she tried to project nonchalance. She wouldn't give her father cause to remind her how to treat Rick again. "I'm sorry to have held everyone up. Yes please. I'll have a sav blanc, but how about we take our drinks through to the table?"

Rick held up a bottle of white. "I'll bring the bottle and a glass for Geilis."

Her parents sat in their usual seats. Rick set a glass of wine on her coaster, filled a glass for himself and sat in the chair opposite hers. She concentrated on her dinner plate, adding little to the conversation until her father mentioned their new security measures.

"I don't know if it's overkill, but I've been looking into the cost of getting security cameras and movement sensors installed. What do you think, Gei?"

Pausing to collect her thoughts, she sipped her wine before answering. "We've never had problems before now. Once we catch our intruder, any extra expenditure on security is likely to be a waste."

"I don't know, Gei. What if, just to take one example, your mother and I were away on business or on holiday and it was only you here by yourself? Wouldn't you feel safer knowing you had a system linked to a security service? I'd sure feel a whole lot better knowing you were protected."

"Are you and Mum thinking of taking a holiday? Where to?" The suggestion had come out of the blue. How long had her parents been contemplating the idea? Of course they deserved a break, especially after her father's heart problems, and Geilis felt perfectly capable of keeping the business ticking over while they took one. Her gaze tried to slide past Rick, but snagged on his injury and a sense of foreboding slithered down her spine. Being alone and isolated from her nearest neighbours by the vineyard and cow paddocks, what would *she* do if confronted by another intruder?

"We're just throwing ideas around at the moment. But we need to take steps to address future possibilities." Her parents' gazes connected, held, and Geilis had the strange feeling there was more behind those looks than they were sharing.

"Well, if you *were* thinking about going on a holiday which, by the way, you richly deserve, I'd have to consider taking on another staff member to—" Like a spider's web the trap her parents had spun closed around her. They wanted to hire Rick permanently, bring him on to help her while they went off on that holiday she'd just agreed they should take. Across the roast pork, feeling angry and cornered, she glared at him.

His expression gave nothing away and she couldn't be sure if—perhaps—he'd somehow engineered the situation.

"No, on second thoughts, I can't imagine needing to hire permanent staff. We have enough part-timers to cover things, and Dad will be back in the vineyard soon. I'll manage until then. After all, we have *Rick* helping out until your arm is mended, Dad. He's the muscle, but no one knows wine and winemaking like you do. You're irreplaceable. And once your arm is mended and you've had a holiday, we'll go back to the way we were.

"Of course we're all grateful that Rick is able to step in and help while you recover, but we all know it's temporary. Anyone like seconds?" Sure she'd neatly cut off any suggestion of Rick remaining beyond the time her father needed to heal, her appetite returned and she scooped another slice of pork and a roast potato onto her plate and liberally covered both with gravy.

***

Annoyed by Geilis' less than subtle reminder of his temporary status Rick strode back to the shearers' quarters. It was pointless to take umbrage; everything she said was true, but it irked him. She didn't want him around. She'd told him point blank and then hammered it home over dinner. He changed into dark clothing and sat reading a spy novel until close to ten o'clock, and then turned out the lights.

Sitting in the dark, his eyes adjusted to the low light while he planned the route for his first security check. The most vulnerable part of the winery was the cellar where the casks of wine were stored. He would focus on that part of the business for a start. The sliced water pipe highlighted a vulnerable aspect that, alone, he couldn't monitor with absolute certainty. Reg's suggestion of movement sensors was sensible, even if they were triggered by wildlife.

Armed with a heavy torch, Rick slipped out the back door and made a wide detour along the tree lined perimeter before cutting back to the winery buildings. Heavy cloud worked in his favour, hiding the waning moon and his movements. But the same conditions would also favour an intruder.

Rick trod softly, staying close to buildings and pausing often to listen. Thirty minutes later, satisfied with his first circuit, he unlocked and slipped through the side door of the tasting area and through the kitchen towards the office. While Reg's offer of accommodation in the shearers' shed was thoughtful, it was too far away if another intrusion occurred. In the office, he would hear anyone attempting to break into the cellar.

Despite its short and narrow confines, the camp bed beckoned. Rick turned the doorknob. A soft breath to his right, the sense of a presence in the room warned him. His thumb hit the button of his torch as he pushed the door wide and, knowing where the attack would come from, he reached for the intruder.

He caught a fleeting glimpse of his attacker and a familiar floral scent before a heavy wrench descended—a swish of air flittered across his skin as the downward arc missed his head by a hairsbreadth.

Geilis!

He grabbed her wrist and twisted the wrench from her grasp. She stumbled and one hand shot out, connecting with his jaw. He tipped his head away from her hand. "It's me, Geilis. Trying to give my egg an egg of its own, are you?"

Geilis slitted her eyes in the glare of torchlight and gripped his shirt before he lowered the torch. "Damn it. You gave me a fright creeping in like that. Aren't you supposed to be doing your rounds outside?"

"Winery security, your father said. No boundaries. I take that to include the casks of wine as well as everything outside."

Her hand relaxed its grip on his shirt and her breathing settled into a steadier rhythm, but she didn't move away. "You don't need to worry about the cellar. I'm sleeping in the office. That way, I'll hear if someone breaks in. I never expected *you* to come inside."

"I figured on sleeping on the camp bed. After last time I reckon the casks are the most vulnerable items if someone really wants to harm the winery's stock."

She tipped her head to the side and frowned. "Actually the vines are most important, more than the finished product."

He thought for a moment and then nodded. "Because they represent all future vintages?"

"Got it in one." She looked at her hands pressed against his chest and lowered them quickly as though she had forgotten how close she was standing to him. Was that good? Or terrible?

Certain she didn't see him as any kind of *safe* option, inspired by the darkness around them, a flash of devilment sparked in him. He flicked the switch on his torch, plunging them into darkness.

"What is it? Did you hear something?" Geilis' hand smacked onto his chest and the faint scent of flowers, warmed by her body, drifted to his nose. He covered her hand with his. Her breath hitched and beneath his fingers, her pulse skittered.

He lowered his head, and his voice. "No, but I don't want to advertise our presence if anyone comes calling tonight. The light is a dead giveaway."

"Oh, of course."

"Now about this idea of yours of sleeping in the office—"

"I'll be perfectly safe. I'll lock the door and keep my phone in my hand."

"But if the door is shut, how well do you think you'll hear an intruder?"

"I heard you."

"I opened the door. And you missed me with your wrench. What would have happened if I'd been the intruder?"

"You're not."

"But if I was—how would you call for help if I tied you up and gagged you?" Better not let his imagination go there. "You're playing with fire."

"Just because I missed, you don't think I can handle myself against an intruder. I'm plenty able to disarm a man."

Including him, although not in the way she meant. But Geilis didn't seem to know how beautiful—how *disarming*—she was. Or how her nearness as they whispered their conversation aroused him. The brush of her breath across his cheek, her scent—floral mixed with mint toothpaste and the unique scent that was Geilis. Even blindfolded he'd pick her out of a line up. If he turned his head a little he would find her sassy mouth. Kissing her would be the simplest way to end this conversation, but he liked talking with her, even if most of their exchanges bordered on argument. "But not when you advertise your presence as they're coming through the door."

"I didn't."

"Your perfume is a dead giveaway and I heard you breathing. I sensed your arm moving, but I knew a cosh on the head was the likeliest form of attack."

Faint illumination leached through partially open slimline blinds and, as his eyes adjusted to the dim light, he saw her frown, and the curiosity in her gaze. "How? How do you know these things?"

He shrugged. "Instinct. I learned bushcraft from—a friend. It was useful in prison." A number of times it had saved him, although he hoped one day he'd forget the last six months.

"Prison must have been awful."

Like a bucket of cold water in mid-winter, any thought of kisses died as the nightmare of the past six months washed over him. She would never know how bad it could be. At least he'd saved Harvey from that knowledge. But his muscles tensed, coiled ready to respond as memories of close calls and aggressive inmates raced through his brain. The knuckledusters, the fear of turning his back in the showers, the shiv one inmate had fashioned from a toothbrush he'd hidden. Rick's lungs constricted and he tried to locate *normal* but it had flown at Geilis' words. "Yeah, not somewhere I plan on returning. Look, why don't you go to bed. I'll doss down here— with the doors open so I hear if a bad guy tries to break in." It would be hours before his mind clamped a lid on the maelstrom of memories. Hours before his muscles unclenched.

"Why did you tense up when I mentioned prison?"

He spoke around a tight throat. "I didn't."

"You did. It must have been bad." Her palms settled on his chest and he felt the heat of her body intensify and fuse with his.

Darkness, and nobody around were a bad combination. In the dark his other senses reached out and exaggerated Geilis' nearness; her scent and the feel of her hands sliding slowly up his chest; her choppy breaths across his cheek. Without meaning to his free hand slid around her waist. In the space of mere seconds her presence dimmed the nightmare past and grounded him in the here and now. If only he could claim the reprieve of her lips. His head lowered and hers tipped up.

"Can I keep you company?" No more than a whisper separated her mouth from his.

Frustration rose in him. Did she think he couldn't cope with his memories? With talking about jail? Or was this about Geilis, aware of her power over him and using it to get her own way?

He raised his head and gripped her shoulders. "Why? Either you trust me to do the job your father hired me to do, or you don't. Which is it, Geilis?"

"I trust you. I told you before, only—"

"I'm the *muscle* you hired, remember? I don't need you keeping an eye on me. I don't want you here. You say you trust me. Go back home and leave the security of *your* vineyard to me."

She huffed and tension quivered through her slim shoulders at his dismissal. "Fine. Let me go and damned well keep yourself company."

"And Geilis—"

"What?"

"Don't slam the door on your way out."

Chapter Eleven

Her legs were bound. Geilis couldn't move, couldn't stop Rick disappearing into a red pixelated mist.

Come back, please. I believe you . . .

The clatter of dishes intruded and Geilis blinked, looking down at the sheet wrapped around her legs. Sunlight streamed through her bedroom window, the angle telling her she'd slept in. She threw the sheet back and looked at her clock. Six-thirty! She never slept in, never slept so late that her staff would have begun work without her. Without stopping for a shower, she pulled on a pair of jeans and a long-sleeved T-shirt, dragged her hair into a low ponytail and raced out the front door.

Work was well underway in the vineyard by the time she made an appearance. Even Rick, damn the man, looked as though he'd slept the night through. Her father was in the office checking orders when she knocked on the door. She cast a furtive glance at the neatly-made camp bed as though it might hold the imprint of Rick's athletic body. How pathetic was that? He'd told her to get out, that he didn't need her, didn't want her around while he kept watch over *her* vineyard. Doing the job they were paying him to do, for goodness sake, so why was she grumpy with him? It wasn't his fault she'd been seduced by the night and his nearness and given free rein to her wayward imagination.

Her father looked up from the pages in his hand and she smiled, a fond not-a-care-in-the-world daughterly smile and kissed his forehead. "Coffee, Dad?"

"Yes thanks. And maybe we can talk before you head onto the terraces."

"About what? Has something happened? Is there a problem with the orders? I checked them yesterday and—" Her empty stomach flipped and contracted and her brain raced back over the administrative tasks she'd tackled yesterday. What had she missed? What—

"Nothing wrong, sweet pea. Just, I think we should discuss the direction we want to take Romney Wines."

Relief shouldn't have stolen her breath, but even with her father available to consult, any tiny fault in her performance was exaggerated in her mind. Her work had to be perfect—*she* had to be perfect to take on responsibility for her father's life's work. One day she was going to add her stamp to it—one day. But a discussion was a great start.

"I'll put the kettle on." Discussing their future direction sounded like her father was happy to have her as more than a temporary manager while his arm healed. Discussion suggested the possibility of bringing some of her ideas to fruition under Dad's expert eye. Glad that she'd stopped by the office before she headed out, her confidence was high as she set two mugs of coffee on the desk.

Her father closed his laptop and swivelled to face her. He sipped his coffee and smacked his lips. "Ah, you make a good cuppa, Gei. Nothing beats a coffee first thing."

Geilis' stomach gurgled and she thought ruefully of her missed breakfast. But confessing to her father she'd slept in wasn't going to happen. Instead she grinned. "Unless it's a Romney wine last thing."

"Hmm, nice tagline. Could be the beginning of a new campaign."

"I can play with it if you like, see what I can come up with, especially if you're thinking about changing direction."

Taglines... beginnings... Dad's words sounded as though change was in the air. She sipped her coffee and waited for her father to work his way up to whatever he wanted to discuss. Work could wait a little longer. This morning, this moment, felt too significant to rush.

"I've been talking with your mother about where we're positioning ourselves in the market, and we believe, with the right promotion, we can capture more of your generation's market share. But to do that, one of us needs to get involved in more research and meeting with our distributors."

"Is that why you and Mum were talking about being away from the winery for a while?" Sipping her coffee, she waited for the caffeine high to catch up to the pleasure of the chat with her father.

He chuckled and leaned back in his chair. "You saw right through our subterfuge. With Rick here to help and keep an eye on the place at night, we feel reasonably comfortable with the idea of heading off on our fact-finding tour. What do you think? Ideas, suggestions, contacts from your course?"

Keeping Rick around was a two-edged sword. He made her feel safe, but at the same time, his presence sent dangerous thrills down her spine. She sat straighter on her seat and sternly thrust thoughts of Rick into a mental strongbox and slammed the lid. "As a matter of fact I do have a couple of friends who can help on the advertising side. We shared ideas and they were on the same page as me." Claire and Ronan had even sketched out a new label for her one night over a bottle of Romney wine. "So, do you have an image in mind for our wine?"

"I'm open to suggestions."

"Okay. I'll keep thinking about possibilities and tonight, I'll show you the label my friends made. I came up with the concept during one of my final year subjects. It might be a good starting point." By the time she joined the staff working around the vineyard, her imagination was buzzing.

When Katy rang late in the day, Geilis couldn't hold back her excitement. She sat on the patio steps in the shade and shared her good news. "Dad's really happy for me to add my ideas, and Katy, I'm sure we can use this to put Romney Wines on the major tourist trail. Once the pioneer museum has made the move to Lark Creek we'll have a good combination of places and events to start promo; and we can link back to Travis' country Christmas."

Katy was as enthusiastic as Geilis. "And forwards to the next one. Gei, that's wonderful news. I'd love to see the new label."

"Nothing's definite yet but I'm optimistic."

"The next generation of Romney wine, brought to you by Geilis Romney. Wow, you'll be famous!"

"Don't know about that, but between us we'll put Lark Creek back on the map. Oh, Katy, it feels great knowing Dad trusts me enough to bring me on board so soon after finishing my degree. I thought I'd be apprenticing for a few more years before I got a say." She could almost taste her dream coming to life.

"Well, doing it with the safety net of your dad's guidance is the best possible training. You're lucky. I stumbled blindly through the renovation of Gran's home and researched B and B's online until I fell asleep at the computer. It was more good luck than anything that it worked."

"But you're not alone, Katy. Not now."

"I know, but things were pretty rocky between Travis and me before Christmas. Now . . . Gei, keep it secret, but Travis is going to record a new album."

Geilis whooped a cowboy-worthy "Yeeha!" before covering her mouth with her hand and giggling. "Sorry about deafening you. That's great news! Do you know when?" Out of the corner of her eye she saw Rick give her a curious look as he pushed a wheelbarrow full of clippings towards the compost area. Let him think she was crazy. But she lowered her voice. Secrets shouldn't be shared inadvertently.

"Maybe this May. He's been writing new material as though his life depends on it since the concert. It's like he's found a new lease of life."

"He found you, Katy. You inspired him to rejoin the land of the living. Better get back to work. The hired hand is giving me that look again." Rick had merely glanced at her when she whooped as he wheeled the barrow up the slope, but just seeing him had distracted her.

"Do you mean Rick? Doesn't sound like him. Okay, catch up over the weekend?"

"Sure. I'll call in to Rose Cottage." There was nothing like a girlfriend chat to lift her spirits. As she slipped her phone into her pocket, Rick appeared pushing the empty wheelbarrow towards the work shed.

He set the barrow down at the bottom of the steps and removed the cap he'd taken to wearing while his forehead was swollen. One tanned forearm wiped the sweat from his brow before he looked at her with dark, enigmatic eyes. "That was the last load of clippings. I've checked the new drip lines are working properly. Is there anything else you need before I head home for a shower?" All day he'd kept his distance and their interactions had been businesslike, not at all like the remnant of emotion she'd woken with. The memory of their almost-kiss in the dark unsettled her. If only she could remember what her dream of Rick had been about.

Glancing at the barrow, she shook her head before meeting his gaze. Over the past few days working alongside Rick, she had begun to expect the unexpected—a subtle joke, a thoughtful observation, a challenge to her perspective. But last night he'd clammed up like a mollusc protecting a pearl and today he'd been the perfect employee, respectful and—not unfriendly precisely, but distant. Exactly like he treated the other employees.

For goodness sake, she'd been sympathising with him last night, but as soon as she mentioned prison . . .

That's why.

The realisation rocked her. Rick was self-contained; he didn't want sympathy from anyone, especially not her. How could she have been so insensitive? But there'd been a moment last night when they'd forgotten they were employer and employee. A moment when the darkness closed in around them and Rick held her shoulders and whispered in her ear. Not sweet nothings—that wasn't his style—but his nearness had turned her thoughts to sharing more than a night watch with him.

And I went and mentioned prison and threw cold water over any hope of that.

"Geilis?"

"What?" Surprised at finding herself standing beside him when she'd been sure there'd been several metres between them, she blinked rapidly. "Oh—no, nothing else. Thanks."

What the hell was wrong with her? Heat surged through her body and she turned on her heel and strode away. Once around the corner she slumped against the wall and slapped her hands over heated cheeks.

Get. A. Grip.

Geilis Romney was not going to fall for any man, let alone one whose actions had disappointed the image she had of him. By committing theft, Rick had let her down. She had respected his work ethic and quiet help for people like Merle

Leonard and he'd broken that trust. He wasn't the man she thought he was, but still—*he's a good man in most ways.*

Brett's voice intruded on her thoughts, his sneering tone full of malice. "The con is trying to get into the pants of the owner's daughter. What—you think she'll sleep with you because you're a suck up? Everyone knows you're no good." Pressed against the cool stone, Geilis edged closer, stopping near the corner, and peered around.

"Go home, Brett. The work day's over though in your case, *work day* is a misnomer. More like work hour, skiving off like you do." A small movement drew her attention to Rick's right hand. The third finger tapped an agitated rhythm against his thumb, but Rick's neutral tone was almost lazy, as though Brett behaving like an arsehole amused him. Was Brett deliberately trying to provoke Rick, or was he letting a nasty streak show?

Is this what Rick has to put up with every day? Does everyone treat him this way? Indignation swelled in her breast. Not everyone. Her father had never treated Rick with the lack of respect Brett was dishing out. Shame filled her for those odd times when Rick had misinterpreted her behaviour as slurs on his character. She hadn't meant them, had never intended to treat him as somehow less because he'd spent some time in prison.

Or had she, subconsciously?

Had her disappointment with him leached through into her manner? Or was it more about trying to quell the attraction she felt? Before she knew what she was going to say she walked around the corner. "Oh, glad I caught you, Brett. You didn't finish stacking the crates that came in. Why?"

***

Rick's stomach took a dive. It was one thing for Brett to have a go at him in private, but the chance that Geilis had heard his crude reference to her challenged his self-restraint. He gripped the handles of the wheelbarrow so hard his knuckles turned white. Edwards would lock him in a cell at the mere hint of a fight. As much as he longed to teach Brett some respect for Geilis, was it worth going back to prison for?

Breathe deep, son.

Yes, Mum. I'm breathing.

Dull red flared in Brett's cheeks and his expression turned from sneering to surprised embarrassment. He began his shuffle dance, sidling closer to the end of the patio. Rick could almost hear the cogs whirring in his brain, hear the excuses building. "I—uh—might have pulled a muscle. In my back. It, ah, slowed me down."

"Is that so?" She said no more but simply waited, arms loosely crossed over her chest. Her expression gave nothing away. Silently he applauded her restraint. She was so composed, so calm, so . . .

Out of the corner of his eye, he studied her body language, her expression. Maybe not so calm if he was right about the look in her eyes. Fierce, righteous anger burned bright, and Rick was glad it wasn't turned on him.

"I'll—ah—finish it now before I leave." Brett threw a nasty look Rick's way before walking quickly to the rear loading dock.

Geilis watched him go. "There's nothing wrong with his back. Look at him—he's almost running." She turned back to Rick and her angry green gaze pinned him. "What do you know about Brett's *skiving off*?"

Rick relaxed his grip on the wheelbarrow, thankful she'd only caught his comments, not Brett's insinuations about her. He promised himself he'd give Brett no reason to make crude insinuations about Geilis. "Just that I found him having smoko in the shed before break time."

"And you didn't think to tell me or my father?" Her direct gaze belied the cool tone of her voice.

Telling Geilis about how his encounter with Brett had panned out would be like adding fuel to the inflammatory remarks he'd worried she'd overheard. He shrugged. "I reminded him when breaks were and encouraged him to work while he waited for his phone call."

"Next time tell me."

"I'm not a dobber."

She frowned. "If he's smoking inside the shed that's a workplace health and safety issue, not dobbing. Get it?"

"Got it." Gei had a point. There was a line between maintaining safety and dobbing. Brett had crossed it when he smoked around chemicals. "Now you're aware of the infringement."

"Well then—thanks. See you at dinner." She turned and climbed the steps two at a time. The door banged behind her before he thought to ask what she'd thanked him for. Rick shook his head and wheeled the barrow back to the shed.

Women!

By the time he'd showered and dressed for dinner, he was no closer to working out what Geilis' thanks meant.

She can't have heard what Brett said. But she had heard his reference to skiving off. Rick hoped that was all she'd heard. Because sitting across the dinner table from her while the suggestion he was trying to get into her pants played on her mind would be uncomfortable.

But the truth was that, in another time and place, Rick would have had the confidence to pursue Geilis. He liked her. A lot. In the time before he'd gone to jail he might have had a chance with her. He'd never lacked women wanting to go out with him. Jail had knocked more out of him than just his self-confidence. For God's sake, he knew he wasn't guilty and yet here he was thinking he wasn't good enough for Geilis. And he wasn't.

Because the truth sat there, ugly and stark—he had been in jail.

In anyone's book, regardless of the reason, he was bad for business.

Chapter Twelve

The weekend stretched ahead of Rick as he climbed three-quarters of the way to the top of the saddle-shaped O'Reilly's Ridge and stopped. His breathing was still easy, but where the bush track skirted a trio of boulders was his favourite outlook. Resting his daypack on the boulder perched closest to the steep drop off, he drank in the view. Below him, sunlight shimmered in sparkling flashes on the creek, and the sloping hill that led up to Thornyhill Farm on the far side of the valley lay indolent beneath a summer haze.

All week he'd been looking forward to heading bush. Up here, he felt truly free. No covert glances or snide remarks. Just him and the sounds of the Australian bush. He tipped his head back.

Clear summer sky arced above the eucalypts and the heat of mid-morning intensified the scents of the leaves. Eucalyptus and baking granite, the two smells he associated with . . .

"I wondered when you'd get around to visiting again. Heard you coming up the scree slope." The deep voice of Graham Muggeridge preceded his appearance a little way up the curving track.

"I hoped I'd surprise you. Must have lost condition while I was away."

"You couldn't have advertised your arrival more clearly if you'd played reveille on the way up. You'll have to do a whole lot better than that if you want to surprise me." Graham turned and headed off the track into the high tree line. Above them, the stony horn of the saddle-shaped hill loomed dark and steep.

Rick followed Graham, taking care to leave as little trace of his passage as possible. Privacy was like gold to his mentor and Rick respected his friend's need for space. If not for Travis' generous offer of accommodation and the job at the vineyard, Rick might have been living like Graham in the bush even now.

That wouldn't have been a bad thing.

But a small part of him disagreed. The part that couldn't get Geilis out of his mind. And what if the damage at the vineyard had nothing to do with his arrival after all? If it *was* some bizarre coincidence, Geilis and her family could be in danger.

"Here." Graham held back a branch of a slim-leafed olive-green bush and Rick stepped through into a small clearing. A rope strung between two low trees supported a simple lightweight camouflage shelter, and a circle of stones marked the fireplace. All Graham's worldly goods were neatly stacked at the back of the tent.

Rick looked around before sitting on a fallen log and lowering his daypack between his feet. "You've moved camp again." He opened the pack, reached inside and withdrew a bottle of whisky.

"Twice, maybe three times since you left town. A new view every few weeks. What's that you've brought?"

Rick handed the bottle to Graham. "For you. It's only from the local bottle shop, but it'll make a change from the home brew you've been making."

"Thanks, but don't diss the home brew." Graham slipped under the canvas and tucked the bottle inside a bush cupboard and came out a moment later with a bottle of clear liquid. He unstoppered the bottle and held it up to the light before passing it to Rick. "I'm expanding. Try my gin."

"Gin?" Rick took the bottle and sniffed the contents, wondering if Graham was joking. Gin with a subtle aroma of the bush teased his nose. He frowned. "Since when have you been a gin drinker? Last time I was here you were brewing your own beer in a cave."

"Taste it. Tell me what you think." Graham sat a short distance away on the upper end of the log. Leaf shadows patterned his face and body, but his attention was on Rick and the bottle in his hand.

Rick drank, concentrating on teasing out the elusive scent underlying the juniper in the gin. "It's got a hint of lemon, but that's not it. Lemon myrtle?"

"Yep. I've been experimenting with bush flavours."

"It's good, really good. But why the change?"

"Why not? I use bush flavourings in my meals, so why not in my drinks? Besides, change is good for a man. Shakes him out of his comfort zone."

"Not all change is good." Rick's fingers curled into fists on his knees. With Graham, he didn't feel the same need to hide his real feelings.

Graham had accepted the troubled teen Rick had been when he appeared in his camp every couple of weeks, had taught him bushcraft and guided him with a light nudge in the right direction. And, in stark contrast to Rick's stepfather, Graham had shown him how a decent man behaved. Strands of steel grey threaded through his dark hair, which was tied in a low ponytail with a piece of string. That and maybe a few more wrinkles were the only changes Rick discerned in his friend.

Graham reached for the bottle of gin and drank before leaning his elbow on his knee. "Given time, even the months you were in jail will take on a different perspective."

"Different, yeah, but good? I can't think of one good thing that will come out of it."

Graham's gaze pinned him and Rick fidgeted. No one else could make him feel so—young. "The reason you chose to go to jail is one. I don't know for sure, but my guess is you're protecting someone. I have my suspicion who it was, but not why you felt you had to do it."

Rick reached for the bottle of gin and sipped. Hedging was the only way around Graham's certainty. He'd spot it a mile away, but it was the only way Rick could think of to avoid lying. No one else—not even Graham living alone up on the ridge—would hear the truth from his lips. Not if Harvey could still be charged. "Why do you think it wasn't me? The police were certain of my guilt."

"Edwards is a tosser. Besides, I know you. It's not in your nature."

"You're a minority of one then."

"Well, there's another good thing. You'll know which people are decent human beings by how they treat you."

Rick thought about the morning Reg Romney had phoned with the offer of work. "*Damned straight I want you working for me, Rick. You're a good man and my Geilis needs someone she can rely on.*"

"*You can rely on me, Reg. That's a promise.*"

"*I know it, son. I'll see you Monday morning, bright and early.*"

A whip bird called through the bush, and near Rick's left boot, a thumb-sized gecko scuttled through the leaf litter. The sound was soft and soothing and some of the tension he'd carried since returning to town eased. "You might have a point."

"And that's all you've got to say on the subject?"

"That's all I've got to say. Moving on . . ."

With the slightest of approving nods, Graham granted Rick's right to his own counsel. "Heard you've had a bit of trouble at the vineyard."

Rick shook his head. "You live up here without a phone or internet or anything and yet you always know what's going on in town. How?"

Graham pushed the cork back into the gin bottle as he stood. "You've got your secrets, I've got mine. Want to see how my new batch of beer is coming on?"

Rick slung his daypack under the shelter of the tent and joined Graham. "Sure. You realise if anyone gets close enough to your cave the aroma of yeast is going to be a dead giveaway?"

"Nobody comes up here these days."

"Scared off by rumours of the mad hermit of O'Reilly's Ridge I'll bet. You set those rumours circulating, didn't you?"

Graham chuckled. "I never give away my secrets. But a well-placed word here and there works a treat. Come on, the beer needs taste testing before it gets any older."

The midday sun beat down on their backs and sweat trickled down Rick's neck as he stopped at the top of the scree-covered slope and chugged a mouthful of water. Graham lowered his backpack, took out a battered thermos and drank. A V-shaped patch of sweat darkened the back of his shirt and, when he tipped his hat up, the greying hair at his temples was dark with moisture, but that was the only indication his friend gave that the sweltering heat could fry an egg. For a middle-aged man, Graham's strides were silent, and he was as agile as a mountain goat ambling up and down the rocks, finding hand and foot holds that even Rick found difficult to spot.

"Check out the view from here, mate." Graham pointed back towards town.

Rick stood on the lip of the narrow ledge and looked out over the valley. A green ribbon of dark trees marked the path of the creek below Travis' farm before it opened up in a lazy bend past the Romney vineyard and the Hamilton's dairy farm. Small figures moved slowly in the heat on both properties, carrying out daily chores. On the southern side of Lark Creek's main street, a man, indistinguishable from this distance, dance-hopped across the shimmering road.

Graham chuckled and nodded in the direction of town. "That will be Andy MacAndrew. He's too tight to buy new thongs while there's a sliver of rubber between him and the bitumen. I'm waiting to see what he does the day his thongs stick to the road.

"And that bloke, coming round the corner of Dicky's fruit and veggie shop, that'll be—"

Rick's gaze slid along the street to a hunched figure. The man paused; a dark shape at the corner of the faded yellow building, he seemed to be checking the coast was clear before crossing the road and disappearing into the heavy shadow under the awnings on the northern side. "Garrett Thomas. Yeah, I'd know him anywhere." Rick's gut clenched at the sight of his stepfather. He dragged his gaze from the man who'd made his early years hell. If he never had anything more to do with the bastard, it would be too soon.

He followed the curving line of the road out of town, keen to focus on something other than Garrett. Across the road from the dairy farm, up the sloping, blond-grass paddock, Anna Wilkins, the arty woman who had moved into the abandoned worker's cottage, strolled down towards the small dam below her home. Stopping at the edge of the dam, she peeled off her outer clothes and Rick glanced at Graham.

"This feels a bit—I don't know. Like I'm a voyeur."

"If you mean Annie, she wears a red bikini."

Rick squinted, just able to make out two tiny strips of red before the woman stepped over the edge and walked into the dam.

Graham drank again from his thermos before slipping it into his pack and zipping it up. "The water's so low she probably gets a mud bath, but she cools off in that dam of hers most days."

Rick lifted his hat and wiped his forehead before slapping his hat back on. "I'm beginning to understand how you know so much about what's happening."

"Yeah. It's funny how removing yourself from the thick of things lets you see the overall picture; who's doing what, and with whom, who wants to keep their visits to the adult shop quiet; or how often a certain bloke calls into the bakery. I see a lot from here, and most of it means nothing. It's just life happening." Graham shrugged his backpack into position on his shoulders and stepped onto a narrow path above the line of scree. "Come on. That beer isn't getting any younger."

##

As Rick entered the clearing through the thick blanket of mid-afternoon heat, a cackle and scratching in the undergrowth warned him they had company. A chicken with dark-barred feathers strutted around the fallen log, pecking at insects in the leaves. At their approach, the chicken began a curiously direct run towards them.

"You've got company." Bemused, Rick stepped out of the chicken's path.

Graham followed Rick into the clearing and scooped up the chook. She nestled into the crook of one arm and clucked contentedly. "This is Jacqueline, Jacky for short."

"When did you get her?"

"Around the time you—left town." Euphemisms from Graham were rare. Like Geilis, he called a spade a shovel.

This careful tiptoeing was more embarrassing than the bald truth. Rick faced his friend. "You said the words before, why not again? I went to jail."

A flash of anger flickered in Graham's eyes and his jaw clamped shut as they faced off. Jacky cackled softly, as though the raised voices disturbed her, and Graham stroked her neck and back. "For a crime you didn't commit. I'd stake all my booze, plus Jacky here, on that being true." Graham's direct gaze challenged Rick to deny the truth of which he seemed so certain.

Rick realised his jaw had dropped when Graham gave him a grim smile. He snapped his mouth shut, his guard up ready to deny it. He had to continue denying it to everyone. If just one person knew the truth for certain, his sacrifice would have been in vain.

"Knew it. You don't have that sort of deceit in you."

"Mention your suspicions and, much as it would pain me to do it, I'd have to shoot you." Rick glared at his friend.

Graham stroked the hen's head and lowered himself into the shade beneath the tent. The chicken settled in his lap. "No danger then, mate. I'd hear you coming and be long gone by the time you made it to my campsite. Besides, I'm a hermit, remember? Nobody visits and I visit nobody."

"Good then. Just so you know. Not a word—to anybody."

If the police knew the truth, it would be worse for Harvey. No matter that Rick might dream of a life free from the 'ex-con' label, that's all it could ever be—a dream.

Chapter Thirteen

Geilis shooed the poddy calf back through the broken fence and looked for a simple means to keep the fallen picket upright while she walked all the way to the work shed, retrieved tools and came back—on the quad bike next time. "I really don't have time for this, little fella, so please, just stay there while I—" She grabbed a branch and rammed it into the hard dirt before angling it towards the picket. It held . . . for all of three seconds before the inquisitive calf nosed at her work. She jumped backwards as both branch and picket fell with dull thuds.

"Drat and double drat."

"Is that worse than a single damn?" Rick's amused voice sounded nearby.

Slapping her hands on her hips she faced him, embarrassment warring with mild relief. If she left the calf while she walked back to the shed, he'd be goodness knew where by the time she got back to the fence. In amongst the vines most likely. "See if you can do better—or, better still, why don't you go back and get tools to fix this while I spend some time explaining to Hughie here why he isn't allowed this side of the fence."

The calf nudged her in the backside and she turned and shooed him back into his paddock. Picking up the fallen picket she tried to hold it in place as the calf mooed in complaint.

"Hughie?" Rick tipped his head and eyed off the calf determinedly pushing against her hand.

"Yeah, like Hugh Hefner. The grass is always greener and all that."

Rick chuckled and his wry grin deepened the crinkles at the corner of his eyes. "He doesn't look old enough to be chasing after your wine grapes. Let's have a look at this post." He dropped his daypack beside her feet and squatted next to the fallen picket. Whether it was the sheer breadth of his shoulders or his male smell Geilis didn't know, but Hughie stood meekly by watching as Rick checked the dirt-encrusted bottom of the fallen pole and then the hole into which it slotted.

"I tried ramming it back in and then I tried using a branch—a makeshift job at best to keep Hughie out—but it needs a heavy-duty mallet to make it hold." Geilis tucked a loose strand of hair behind her ear and dabbed at her sweaty face with the back of her dirty hands.

Rick inserted the picket into the hole and wiggled it. "Was it loose like this when you found it?"

Geilis thought back to the moment she spotted the calf heading through the fallen stretch of fence. "I was more intent on herding Hughie back to his paddock, but . . . I think it was loose when I stood it in the hole. Why?"

"We need to check if any of the others are loose. It might just be that Hughie here has pushed until this picket came loose and once this one is fixed, end of story. Or it could be the dry weather has caused the soil to contract and loosened the picket. If that's the case there are likely to be others ready to fall. I'll do a quick check along this fence line if you go back for tools and the quad bike. Unless you'd rather—"

"I've already battled with Hughie to keep him on his side of the fence. Your turn to babysit."

***

A soft sigh of what Rick took to be relief escaped and Geilis smiled, a genuine I'm-glad-you-showed-up-when-you-did smile that zapped through him like a jolt from an electric fence. He'd watched her efforts to repair the break and hold Hughie back as he strode along the dirt road that ran a couple of hundred metres further on from the single strip of bitumen. The track petered out past the bend and became a steep, rocky scramble, which was why few people bothered climbing O'Reilly's Ridge.

And he'd enjoyed the view as her denim-clad bottom wiggled as she twisted the picket this way and that in a vain attempt to make it stay upright. "Were you trying to screw it into the dirt?"

"It seemed like a good idea when pushing didn't work. Back in ten or so." She strode away, breaking into a jog before she reached the edge of the vines.

Rick turned his attention to the fallen fence, picked up the branch and threaded it through the wires. He thrust the end of the branch into the picket hole with a thud. Eyeing off the calf, he fixed it with a stern look. "No touching that, Hughie-boy, unless you want to find out what prairie oysters mean. Got it?"

The calf mooed as though it understood and trotted away. Before the roar of the quad bike signalled Geilis' return, Rick had checked the length of fence between Romney and Hamilton land. Three other pickets at random intervals were a bit loose. He examined the ground around each. Was there any chance someone had loosened them? Shaking his head, he stood and dusted his hands off on his jeans.

"I've brought a couple of head lamps in case there's more than one picket. We don't have much daylight left." Geilis swung a leg over the bike and unclipped a bucket of tools from the carrier. She reached into the bucket and took out a heavy mallet. "Toss you for it."

"What are we tossing for?" Geilis threw the mallet, handle end up. He caught it near the head.

Geilis set the bucket down and sauntered up to him. Setting one hand above his she wrapped her hand around the handle and grinned. "The right to wield the mallet rather than steady the picket. Your turn."

He eyed off the length of handle. "So if I win I get to hammer."

She set her other hand above his. "Yep. Would now be a good time to tell you I've never lost this?"

Taking a more relaxed grip this time, Rick met her gaze. "Welcome to the first time then."

"You'll never beat me. All I've got to do is fit three fingers on the handle near the top and ..."

Rick spread the fingers of his upper hand on the handle. If he'd judged it right Geilis wouldn't manage two fingers, let alone three.

She wrapped her little finger followed by her ring finger around the handle and exerted pressure, trying to force his hand a fraction lower. "I'm there—almost there—"

"Not a snowflake's hope, Gei." Somehow the game had drawn them closer until only the mallet handle and their bent arms separated them. She must have realised it at the same moment he did because she froze. Two fingers clung to the top of the handle while her gaze collided with his and held. Gently he eased the handle from her grip and turned to the job at hand. Twilight was winning the battle over daylight and they had a bad habit of falling into intimate moments in the dark. Moments that tempted him in ways he couldn't give in to.

"Grab a headlamp and come hold the picket for me. I promise not to miss it." If his voice came out gruffer than intended, he hoped she'd put it down to concern over the waning light.

Without a word she did as he asked, her gaze intent on the picket as she held it steady, leaning away from him. He lined up the metal top with the mallet and swung it over his right shoulder. It landed with a dull thud and the picket sank into the ground with a shudder. Geilis gave it an experimental jiggle. "A couple more whacks like that should do it."

As soon as the picket was solid in the ground, Rick attached the wires into the holders, shouldered the mallet and strode up the hill to the uppermost loose picket. Working in tandem, they secured the fence from top to bottom as the last gold and orange clouds deepened to purple in the western sky.

Low in the east, Venus glowed brighter than any star. Geilis packed the tool bucket and put it into the carrier, switched off her head lamp and tossed it in on top of the tools. "Want a ride back to your quarters?"

"Thanks. Will you let your mother know I'll be late for dinner?" He slung his daypack over one shoulder and climbed on behind Geilis. Beneath the scent of work-warm skin, a hint of flowers greeted him, lingering on the air even as she leaned forward to give him more space. He had no idea what the scent was, but he'd forever associate it with Geilis.

"Sure."

Resolving not to touch her, Rick held himself as far away as humanly possible on a shared seat. If she drove smoothly he wouldn't have to touch her, wouldn't have to tighten his muscles to stop from wrapping an arm around her and burying his face in her hair.

His hands tightened on the edge of the seat behind his bottom, but when Geilis started the engine the bike leapt forward like a kangaroo bounding across the plains. Sanity took a detour, self-preservation kicked in and his arms wrapped around her waist as the bike bounced into every hole in the paddock. Geilis' body tensed at his touch, but by the time she eased to a stop in front of his quarters, her back was pressed against his chest and flyaway strands of hair tickled his nose.

Neither said a word. Geilis tipped her head and half-turned, exposing the lightly tanned length of her neck, pale in the yellow sensor light.

Rick wasn't made of steel, and damn if her quiet breaths and softly parted lips weren't an invitation. He bent his head and touched his mouth to warm skin, breathing in the scent of her. A soft indrawn breath escaped, and she tipped her head further, granting him access, giving him permission to continue. Uncaring if she recognised the power she had over him at this moment, he tightened his hold around her waist and pulled her rounded bottom into the angle of his legs. Pleasure and pain shot through him in equal measure as she leaned her head on his shoulder and pushed her bottom back against him. Their mouths meshed and beneath his hungry lips, hers demanded satisfaction.

Soft lips parted and she lightly nipped his lower lip. Her kisses stole every thought from his head. He groaned. Who was giving whom satisfaction became a moot point as her tongue touched his, teasing, tempting, until his hands slid down ready to lift her across his lap. His fingers wrapped around the soft curve of her hips, pressed in.

Beneath one of his hands, Geilis' phone rang.

Reality intruded, vibrating beneath his arm.

Her eyes opened slowly, as lost as he had been. She blinked, stared at him as though unsure what to do, and then sighed. "That will be Mum wondering where I am. I'd better get back to the house."

Biting off a grunt of frustration, he swallowed his disappointment. "I'll be there as soon as possible. Will you tell her please?" The last thing he wanted to do was to let Geilis go, but he forced himself to get off the bike and step away.

Geilis nodded and revved the engine. "I'll tell her." She took off without a backward glance.

He watched until the bike disappeared behind a line of trees that separated the main house from the old sheep paddock and then dumped his gear on a spare bunk. Toeing off his boots, he stripped off his clothes and wrapped a towel around his waist. In lieu of another twenty-k run, a cold shower was more than a way to clean off the day's sweat and dirt.

After that ride behind Geilis, it was a necessity.

Chapter Fourteen

An occasional breeze drifted across the vineyard carrying the smell of fruit and a tang of sluggish creek water. Low in the western sky, the waning moon hung like a horned Viking helmet, marking the passage of two weeks since Rick had started work with Geilis' family.

And a week of frustrated distraction since he kissed me.

It seemed impossible so little time had passed when so much had happened. Their intruder hadn't returned since Rick had been injured, and Geilis was beginning to relax into the rhythm of their shared security routine. Maybe relax was too casual a word. Rick remained at least two steps from her as they did their rounds.

She checked the loading bay door was secure while Rick locked the side door into the cellar. She rattled the lock before turning to Rick. "Do you think we've heard the last of him?"

"The intruder?"

"Yes." Her reply snapped out, terse with frustration since those brain-scorching kisses the afternoon of Hughie's incursion. She'd even deliberately kangaroo-hopped the quad bike a couple of times yesterday and given him the opportunity to hold her again, but his touch had been impersonal.

"Maybe. But I won't relax our routine just because he hasn't been back for a while." Rick removed the key from the lock. It jangled as it slid down and joined the others on the ring. "Stay vigilant, stay safe. That's the motto."

She dragged a breath into her suddenly tight chest. "You think he's biding his time?" Time might eventually dull the knot that tightened in her stomach when she recalled the attack, but the image of Rick, slumped and bleeding, hadn't dimmed. If anything it was sharper than ever in her memory, and the reason she accepted his presence on their nightly rounds. If not for that memory, she would prefer only the company of her own thoughts and the kind of peace Rick's absence allowed her to wallow in since it seemed unlikely she'd be treated to a repeat of his kisses.

"I don't know. All I'm saying is it's important to maintain vigilance. If he's an opportunist, he may have given up because we've made the winery too difficult a target. Let's wrap this up. Your mother's expecting us back for dinner."

"Hungry for lasagne, are we?"

"Hungry for everything your mother serves up. She's a great cook."

"Do you cook?" She climbed onto the quad bike and inserted the key into the ignition. Self-preservation warred with a perverse desire to provoke him into a repeat of kisses she hadn't been able to forget. Sanity won and she sat as far forward on the seat as she could.

Rick joined her, holding onto the seat behind his bottom as she eased the bike forward. Since their post-Hughie kiss, the distance he'd maintained between them had sent a clear message—he wasn't interested in her. Not in *that* way.

And she—contrary woman that she was—didn't want him to be interested in her. No matter that the memory of his mouth trailing over her neck set flutters loose in her stomach. Her goal for the winery demanded all her attention and creative energy. Rick was a distraction she didn't need. Didn't want.

But damn it, I want more of that crazy intense high his kisses gave me.

"Everything okay?" His chest bumped her shoulder as he leaned forward and his warm breath skated past her ear.

Her muscles tensed at the brief connection. "Of course. Why?"

"You sighed."

"If I did it's only that I'll be glad when Dad realises I can do security rounds all by myself. I don't need a minder." It grated that Dad had agreed to Rick's suggestion because the break in had worried him, but it felt like her father didn't completely trust her.

No, I'm not being fair. He's worried because he's not able to do everything and has to delegate.

"Of course you don't."

"So how about you let me do this round alone in future. Dad doesn't need to know."

"Can't do that."

"It won't be a problem. We just don't say anything. What he doesn't know can't worry him. Tomorrow I'll do the early check and you can do the late-night round. Deal?" Wanting him to agree, afraid he might do just that, she bit her lip as she waited for his response.

"No. I promised your father I'd do the job. I won't lie to him. I'm surprised you're even considering it."

Was that censure in his voice?

How dare he?

"I'm surprised telling a little white lie matters to *you*."

Behind her she felt his body tense and he was silent for several heartbeats as the bike slowed and she pulled up at her front gate. Rick stepped off the quad before she'd even turned off the engine and took a few steps, stopping with one hand on the picket gate.

His body rigid, Rick's free hand curled into a fist and her heart sank. That barb was beneath her. After two weeks, surely she knew him better than that. Her voice struggled to get past a lump of regret blocking her throat. "Rick, I didn't mean—"

Half turning his head, he flung a terse reply in her direction. "It matters." Then he pushed through the gate and let it bang shut behind him.

Over dinner and a Romney Shiraz, Geilis tried to relax and join in the conversation her parents and Rick were engaged in, but her concentration ebbed when Rick's gaze connected with hers. Knowing her unfair comment on the drive to the house had hurt him, she'd expected anger. The hint of vulnerability surprised her. She rested her elbows on the table and leaned on her folded hands. Were there flecks of gold in his dark chocolate eyes, or was that some trick of the light? He broke the connection and turned away, responding to some comment her father made.

Why had she allowed her frustration with everything— scratch that, with him—to leach into their conversation? Hurting Rick with that innuendo about his character was wrong on every level. She would apologise before he left.

And mean every word of it.

Picking up her glass, she sipped the wine and pondered why Rick Peyton, a criminal who had cheated and stolen from people they both knew, who had behaved so badly even his stepfather appeared to have disowned him, could stir and intrigue her. He was the town's black sheep and yet . . .

Everything he'd done since he'd arrived at the vineyard contradicted her expectation of him. But not what she'd thought of him before his crime came to light. Which was the real Rick? Was there a reason other than greed behind what he'd done?

She touched her tongue to the corner of her mouth, catching a drop of wine. Rick's gaze fastened on her mouth and his eyes darkened. If she didn't know better, she could forget that he hadn't willingly touched her, that he'd actively avoided her; she could imagine that, maybe, she stirred a similar reaction in him.

"What do you think, Gei? Would you be happy with that?" Her mother's question caught her attention and she turned to see her mother, fork raised halfway to her mouth, watching her.

"Sorry, what was that?"

Her mother glanced at Rick and grinned before meeting Geilis' eyes. "If your father and I head off next weekend, would you feel comfortable holding the fort here?"

"We won't be gone long. A week at most, but we want to meet Gervais Armand. He'll only be in Brisbane for a couple of days." Her father set his cutlery on his empty plate and leaned back.

"Armand—he's the Loire Valley label, isn't he?" She picked up her glass and drank to hide her heated cheeks and the flush crawling down her neck.

Her father nodded and reached for the wine bottle. "That's the one. Our original vines came from his family's vineyard and we want to explore ways to link with his label."

"Reg, the doctor agreed to you having *one* glass a day after yesterday's appointment. One *glass*, darling, not one bottle." The warning note in her mother's voice was gentle, but unmistakeable, and her father set the bottle down with a rueful smile.

Geilis glanced at her mother before turning to her father. "I didn't notice you were allowed to drink again, Dad. That's good news, isn't it?"

"I guess so. When the wine is as good as ours, it's easy to forget. It slips so smoothly over the palate. Are you sure you gave me a full glass, love? I swear I've only had a half one." He looked at his wife with a hopeful expression.

Seeing her father more like his old self, hearing the gentle banter between her parents, gave her confidence in Dad's full recovery. "I'll give you the phone number and address of my university friends, if you have time to meet with them. They're teaming up with a PR consultant who might have some ideas how we can target our new market segment."

"Excellent." Her father rubbed his hands together and reached for his empty glass. He looked hopefully at his wife. "Now, if only I had a drop of wine to toast the progress of Romney Wines."

"Nice try, Reginald." Geilis' mother pushed her chair back from the table and walked around to her husband. She kissed his cheek before clearing his plate. "We'll have plenty to celebrate later."

"That we will." He took hold of her free hand and they leaned in to one another, their foreheads touching. A lump formed in Geilis' throat as she watched her parents. After all the years they'd been married, they were still in love.

***

Rick stood, reached over and took Geilis' plate, and stacked it on top of his. "Is there anything else you want me to do while you're away, Reg?"

"You're doing enough now, but I'll feel much better knowing you're nearby while we're gone." He patted Geilis' hand and squeezed it affectionately.

Geilis covered his hand with her free one and gave him a mock frown. "Dad, I'm not a little girl anymore. I can take care of myself."

"I'll do what I promised, Reg." He flicked a glance at Geilis. Her eyes widened and for a brief moment, her gaze pleaded with him. No matter how much she wanted to ditch his company, he wouldn't allow her to lie to her father about the daily security check. But she'd put him in his place with that crack about him not minding telling a lie. He'd thought she was different from the others. Was the truth that she couldn't see beyond his time in jail to who he really was? His gut clenched and bile burned his throat.

Digging deep, he tried to find comfort in his mother's mantra. Once, it had been enough. Once, it had done the trick. But Geilis Romney, with her barbed comments, had put him in his place as thoroughly as jail had held him.

Jillian wrapped an arm across her daughter's shoulders. "Hate to tell you, but you'll always be our little girl, even when you're old and grey."

As Rick watched the closeness of the Romney family, he rubbed a knuckled hand over his chest. Dim memories of dinners with his mother and Harvey when Garrett Thomas had been *away*—their euphemism for his time in jail—flitted through his mind. Happier times when he had been part of a family too. Here, he was the outsider; the ex-con Geilis expected the worst from.

Damn if he would let what she thought of him affect his work here. If she wanted to treat him like that, he wouldn't come to the house for dinner while her parents were away. Keeping his distance while honouring his promise to her father would be a snap. He only had to endure her company for the duration of their security rounds.

His gaze returned to the family tableau before he carried the plates through to the kitchen. How dare she expect him to fall in with her wish to deceive her father? Didn't she know how lucky she was to belong to a loving family?

Hard on the heels of that thought came another; would he ever know that sort of connection again?

Chapter Fifteen

"Mr Donaldson is on a call, Mr Peyton. He'll be with you shortly." Salt and pepper hair framed the pleasant smile of the receptionist in the lawyer's office.

"Thanks for fitting me in on a cancellation." No second-guessing himself; no time to overthink what needed to be done. At least he'd know soon enough if he was on a fool's errand with regard to his mother's will.

He headed over to a comfortable-looking two-seater couch in the lawyer's waiting room and picked out a health magazine from the neat pile of glossies on the coffee table. It was last month's edition, a fact that partially reconciled him to being here. Magazines were a luxury item, as were his plans to build a gin still. He hadn't been able to stop thinking about the unique flavour of Graham's gin, but the idea of making his own had only evolved after his argument with Geilis. He figured while he had a temporary home with rooms to spare, and time on his hands, making gin was a reasonable hobby. One second-hand fermentation vessel and a couple of bits and pieces from eBay later and he had a still set up in a room in the shearers' shed. But now every spare dollar he earned would be needed to pay for legal representation, he regretted the impulse.

How he was going to pay if the lawyer wanted money up front, he didn't know, but the fact he was sitting in the waiting room was entirely due to Travis needling and encouraging him. Last night when he'd visited for dinner, Rick had finally thrown his hands up and capitulated.

"Okay, blast you. I'll call tomorrow and make a time to see him."

Travis had merely nodded and tossed him another beer and they'd sat talking about his new album. It was being produced, thanks in no small measure to the support of Katy.

Rick flipped through to a feature article on nutritionally balanced diets for long-distance runners, but his mind wasn't on food. Since his return, he hadn't been out to the house to see his brother. Harvey hadn't made any effort to contact him either. Was he ashamed of letting Rick take the fall for him, or had he developed the same selfish streak as his father? Garrett Thomas would think Rick weak for shielding his brother and going to prison in his place.

And that was the difference between them. Garrett would do anything to protect himself. He was more likely to throw his own flesh and blood under a bus than take the rap himself. Rick's job was to look out for his brother, no matter what. Knowing he'd made the only possible choice didn't make what he was about to do any easier.

"Mr Peyton? I'm Jack Donaldson."

Rick tossed the magazine onto the pile and stood, holding out his hand to the lawyer. "Yes, Rick Peyton. Thanks for seeing me today. I was only expecting to make an appointment."

"As luck would have it, I had a cancellation. Come on through to my office." Donaldson was in his mid-thirties, his short blond hair professionally trimmed, and he had a no-nonsense manner that Rick appreciated. When they were seated, he gave Rick his full attention. "What can I do for you?"

"My mother, Laura Peyton-Thomas, passed away five years ago. I believe in her Will she left her house to me and my brother, Harvey, but my step-father is refusing to allow me to enter the premises." Bald statements of fact did little to ease the knot in his stomach when he thought of his gentle mother.

The lawyer pulled a yellow pad of foolscap in front of him and picked up a pen. "What was the address of her home?" He noted the details and then met Rick's gaze. "The first thing we need to do is read her Will. Do you have a copy?"

"There was one at home—"

"But you can't access it now?"

"That's right. I've recently been in jail. When I came back to town, my stepfather refused to allow me to set foot on the property, under threat of shooting me." The rifle was registered to Harvey, but Rick was pretty sure it was for Garrett's use.

Jack Donaldson added the details to his notes before meeting Rick's gaze. "That's one heck of a threat. Let me guess, you don't feel you can report it to the police because of your incarceration."

And the fact Edwards would probably sit back and let Garrett shoot him before locking his father up.

He'd be rid of both of us in one go and reckon he'd done the town a favour.

"Let's just say the sergeant and I have never seen eye to eye." Revealing how much Edwards hated his guts was pointless. Besides, the lawyer would probably agree with the police officer if he knew what Rick had been found guilty of. Few people were prepared to look beyond the fact that he was a convicted felon. "He doesn't think much of my stepfather either."

"If you want to leave this with me for now, I'll do the preliminary search for a copy of your mother's Will. If you are indeed a beneficiary, we can proceed from there. One more question though—why have you left it until now to ask? Surely her Will was dealt with after she died?"

For a moment, Rick looked down at his hands, loosely clasped between his knees. When he met the lawyer's eyes, he shook his head. "As soon as her funeral was over I went bush for a couple of months and when I came back to the house, I didn't think anything of it. We just—went on as before, loathing the sight of each other." There hadn't been any reason to doubt his mother had wished to leave her home to her two sons.

"I thought about demanding my stepfather left, but he's my half-brother's father. It—didn't feel right. It was only after I'd been in jail that he refused to let me back in the house."

"How old is your brother?"

"Twenty-four. It's not like Garrett is worried my presence will be a bad influence on a young and impressionable teenager. Nothing like that."

"Garrett, as in Garrett Thomas is your stepfather?" Jack's eyes narrowed before Rick nodded.

"Sadly, yes. You know him?"

"I saw him once, in the Toowoomba court." So Jack knew Garrett had a criminal record, but if he'd acted for him, did that mean he couldn't act for Rick?

The idea of Garrett inhabiting Rick's mother's house just because Garrett had benefitted from this lawyer's services before him sent seismic tremors fuelled by adrenaline rippling through his body. Sure, there were other lawyers, but not in Lark Creek. He wanted action now. He wanted the home his mother had lived in.

He couldn't lose this lawyer—not to Garrett. Neck and jaw muscles felt frozen, but he forced the question out. "Does this mean we have a problem?"

Jack shook his head. "Fortunately for you, I've never represented him or we would have a conflict of interest. I only set up my practice in Lark Creek six months ago. Right." He checked his watch and noted the time on the top of the page of notes. "I'll get onto the search for a copy of your mother's Will today."

Glad for that small piece of luck, Rick sat up straighter. *Now for the tough bit.*

Unprepared for an immediate consultation with Jack Donaldson, Rick had yet to visit the bank manager to ask about a loan. He swallowed his pride. What else could he do, even if asking the question felt like asking for charity? "About your fee—is it possible I can pay it off?"

The lawyer tapped his pen slowly on the notepad before tossing the pen down and standing. He held out his hand. "That will be fine. And I'll get back to you as soon as I have information."

Relieved and with a sense of optimism daring to assert itself, he shook Jack's hand. "I appreciate that. Thanks."

Chapter Sixteen

"Geilis, we're ready to leave. Where are you?" Her father's question sent Geilis scrabbling for a fresh shirt. Her parents always left at the crack of dawn when they made their irregular trips to the capital.

"I'm coming." She managed to do up two buttons as she raced along the hallway, but her shirttail remained untucked as she stopped in front of them. Two suitcases, still looking new after twenty years, sat side by side next to the front door. Clearly her parents needed to get away more often. Geilis pulled a slip of paper from her jeans pocket and handed it to her mother. "Sorry, I was in the bathroom. Here's the phone numbers for Claire and Ronan, and their address. They're expecting you."

She slipped into first her mother's, then her father's arms and hugged them both tightly. "Drive safely and have plenty of rest stops."

Her mother laughed and wiped a thumb across Geilis' cheek. "You don't need my lipstick there. And yes, darling, we'll take it easy. We've got plenty of time."

"Are you sure you'll be okay by yourself?" Dad took her by the shoulders and peered into her eyes.

Was he more protective since his heart attack had reminded him of his mortality, or had his concern for her increased because of the attacks on the vineyard? Unused to seeing vulnerability in her adored father, she gave him another quick, intense hug. "Hey, I always wanted to be the boss some day. Now I'm getting a whole week to try it out. Love you, Dad."

"Love you, sweet pea." With a huff and a sigh, her father released her and picked up both suitcases.

"We'll ring when we get to our motel." With a little chivvying along by her mother, her father stowed the bags and got into the car.

Geilis waved from the veranda until the sedan turned onto the main driveway and disappeared from sight. Folding her arms across her chest, she leaned against a veranda post and looked across the paddock towards the creek.

The sun crested the hill of Thornyhill Farm. Fingers of warmth caressed her cheek and she closed her eyes and tipped her face to the sky. Early morning was her favourite time of day, when the world was fresh and solitude filled her whole being with peace. Revelling in being the only living soul awake in this moment, she opened her eyes. Movement drew her attention to a lone figure she'd recognise anywhere.

Rick.

He was jogging up the hill towards the dirt road that ran past the western corner of the winery. A silver stripe on the back of his vest caught the sun as he turned towards the hills. How often did he run before five in the morning? And why today when they had planned an early start and a long day in the vineyard? But he ran as though trying to catch the wind, with a long, loping stride that ate up the ground before he disappeared around the bend below O'Reilly's Ridge.

Geilis strode inside, letting the screen door slam behind her. "He'd better not be too tired for work after that effort," she said to the empty house.

An hour later she opened the door of the work shed and stepped through into the relative coolness. Intent on getting an early start, she was taken aback to see Rick standing at the pegboard.

He lifted down a small pruning saw and added it to a bucket of tools on the bench top. No smile was offered, but he flicked a glance her way before picking up the bucket and shouldering a mallet, the same one they'd used to fix the fence and keep Hughie out of the back paddock.

"Good morning. Did your parents get away okay?" There was nothing wrong with his manner or his polite enquiry, nothing to complain about, but how she disliked his tone. Ever since her unforgivable gaffe the other night, *impersonal* was their new relationship. It stretched between them like an ocean.

"Morning, and yes. They were on the road before five. So were you, I noticed."

If he was surprised she'd seen him, his expression didn't reveal it. Only his dark eyes watched her warily, as though he didn't quite trust her. The easy camaraderie that had begun to develop between them had disappeared. Rick shifted the mallet and moved to one side so he could go around her. Clearly she'd hurt him more than she realised. Her breakfast roiled in her stomach.

"It's the only time I can fit in training. I'd better get into my first job for the day."

She didn't block his path, but her sideways movement brought him up short. "You run competitively?" Remembering his long, easy strides as he ran up the paddock, it made sense. Lean muscles and not an ounce of fat on him should have told her he was an athlete. "What distance?"

He dismissed her curiosity with a casual shrug. "Long distance."

He twisted the mallet handle round and round as he waited for her to move, but her feet were glued to the floor. They had unfinished business and she wasn't letting him leave until she'd completed it.

As though Rick sensed she had more to say but which he didn't care to hear, he sidestepped, angling to get past her. "I've packed the rest of the equipment for the morning's jobs onto the quad trailer. Is there anything else before I head out?" His neutral tone rang with disinterest and showed his disinclination to chat with her. He sounded fit and ready for the day, and obviously unwilling to let her into any aspect of his life.

Maybe she deserved the wall of reserve he'd thrown up around himself. If someone had impugned her character as she had done to Rick's, she wouldn't have been so restrained. He'd left while she was washing dishes in the kitchen with her mother and her apology was still unsaid.

"Rick, about that comment I made—"

He shook his head, stopping her before she got any further. "Forget it."

"No, I really need to say—"

His gaze slid past her; someone had entered the shed behind her. Turning, Geilis' heart sank as she noted the interest on Brett's face. How much had he heard? She picked up her clipboard, slid the top sheet out and handed it to him. "Hello, Brett. Can you make a start on this list please?"

He glanced at the paper before shoving it into his top pocket. "Sure. So with Reg gone, does that make me your deputy now?" A smirk and a knowing glance at Rick sent a ripple of annoyance through her.

"Actually, Brett, Dad nominated Rick for that position. Besides, it would be awkward given that you're only able to work part-time, but thanks for offering."

Brett's smirk morphed into a snarl. Without a word, he turned and stomped back through the open doorway, slamming the door behind him.

Geilis swallowed and, taking a deep breath, pinned Rick with the weight of all the authority of an heir apparent. "So, Mr 2-IC, you might want to keep an eye out for Brett today."

Rick tipped his head to the side and met her gaze. "Why did you tell him that?" Impassive as he kept his expression, he couldn't hide the spark within his dark eyes. Like a bolt from the blue, understanding hit hard. She'd just told him in the best possible way that she trusted him.

"That you're second in charge, or that Dad said it?"

"Did he?"

Geilis crossed her arms and tipped her head up to meet his gaze. "We want the best person for the job. That's you. I'll be in the office for the next hour or so and then I'll be manning the tasting counter if anyone is looking for me." She left Rick standing, satisfied that she'd got a reaction out of him.

Finally!

The memory of the flash of surprise in his eyes buoyed her spirits. It wasn't quite the apology she'd aimed for, but it might just be the best thing for Rick.

Because, whichever way she looked at it, he *was* the best man.

***

Rick checked his master list against the tasks completed by Grayson and his brother, Greg. Itinerant workers in their early forties, they showed up every January and stayed until the harvest was complete before moving on. Over the course of a couple of decades, they had accrued a shared knowledge about grape growing and the harvest process that impressed Rick almost as much as their uncanny connection.

"Sure you're not twins?" he asked as he ticked off another item.

Grayson grinned. "Why? Is it because—"

"—we finish each other's sentences?" Greg's smile echoed his brother's.

"Nah. Fifteen months between us, but you live with someone all your life—" Grayson began and Greg ended their joint response.

"—you don't need many words. You just know what the other's thinking. You want us to get a head start on set up for tomorrow?"

"Thanks, that would be appreciated." The brothers ambled to the shed with identical steps, leaving Rick feeling confident as his first day overseeing work in the vineyard drew to a close. Given he was the sole occupant of the old shearers' quarters, where did the brothers stay when they worked at the winery? He shrugged—where they stayed was none of his business—and looked for Brett.

A curl of smoke rose from the side of the tin shed and the acrid smell of burning tobacco reached him as he turned the corner. Cigarette dangling from his lower lip, Brett leaned against the corrugated iron side, phone in hand, thumb scrolling up the screen. Brett looked at him, open defiance in his glare. "What? I'm on my break."

"Break finished an hour ago."

"Yeah, well I worked through mine because of the length of that bloody list you gave me. I'm having my break now."

"I'm sure the list *Geilis* gave you was reasonable, but when you finish your break, come and find me."

"I'm not reporting in to you." Brett's lip curled and his eyes narrowed.

Brett could be slack, but Rick had read his employee notes during his shortened lunch break. Before Brett had changed to part-time, he'd worked for Reg ten years full time and managed the crushing process for three of those years. An unspecified family event was noted against his request to reduce his hours, but Reg's notes indicated he was happy with his employee's attitude and work and willing to accommodate the change of work hours. So . . .

Rick continued as though Brett hadn't said anything. "We need to talk about changing up a couple of jobs and you taking on a bit more responsibility while Reg is away."

Brett's narrow gaze widened and he removed the cigarette from his lower lip. "What responsibility?"

"Let's talk work *after* you've finished your break." He nodded at Brett and left him to mull it over. More than most, Rick knew what it felt like to be passed over because someone didn't trust him. Being an ex-jailbird stripped a man of his confidence and his place in the world.

Grateful that Reg had seen fit to offer him this job—and that Geilis trusted him to oversee the vineyard tasks while she filled in for her father at the cellar door—he felt the need to pass it forward. If Brett was willing to oversee the start of crushing once the harvest was in, Rick hoped the responsibility would restore his engagement with his work.

And *that* would make a happier workplace and ease one of his concerns.

Chapter Seventeen

"Thanks for seeing me after office hours." Rick shook Jack Donaldson's hand and stepped through the door the lawyer held open for him. The street lights had come on an hour ago and it was almost fully dark as he entered the law office.

"No problem. I know how long the days are when you're getting ready for harvest." Jack closed and locked the door behind him and indicated Rick should precede him into his office. "I grew up on a farm in the Lockyer Valley so I understand the urgency. Farmers keep long, exhausting hours when their crops are ready to be picked."

Rick had railed against judgements made about him and his family by people who didn't know them, and yet here he was, surprised to learn the lawyer came from a farming family. The thought was a sobering one. Assumptions were easier to make than he'd realised. He cleared his throat before he stated the obvious, and focused on the reality of life on the land. "I'm learning there's a different rhythm to days in the vineyard, but with harvest starting tomorrow and Reg and Jillian away, it's all hands on deck."

Jack sat on the other side of an expanse of wooden desk old enough to qualify as antique, but without the charm of a loved family treasure. Much like the rest of the décor—fifties retro, if one was kind. It said much about Rick's state of mind on his first visit that he was only now seeing the room as though for the first time. "Under the circumstances, I'm glad you were able to make time to see me. I think what I have to say is better communicated face-to-face."

His stomach clenched at Jack's *face-to-face* comment. Did that mean he had no chance of claiming access to his mother's house? And even if Jack had located a copy of her Will and Rick had a snowflake's hope, that was only the first of several expensive hurdles. He curled his fingers into fists and rested them on his thighs, dredging deep to maintain an impassive expression as he faced his lawyer. "Your text said you have news for me?"

"I do. First of all, I located a copy of your mother's final Will which named you and your brother as the main beneficiaries, with a small bequest to her husband—her second husband, that is."

Rick felt the frown tighten his brow as he grappled with the unexpected detail. "Second husband? I thought Peyton was her maiden name. I didn't know Mum had been married before." The revelation hit him in the solar plexus like a power punch from Muhammed Ali. Where space existed for 'father's name' on his birth certificate, a blank rectangle had mocked him all of his life.

But . . . *a first husband who might be his father!*

Had they divorced? Was the man—his father? Was he alive? The idea he might have someone other than his half-brother who shared his genes fizzed through his blood. "Do you have a name—or any details of my mother's first husband?"

"There's no indication of his name on her death certificate, but apparently she left a key to a safety deposit box at the bank. It was meant to be passed on to you after her death. Maybe there's something in the box that will tell you who he is. Or was."

"Do you have it?" Dry-mouthed with the anticipation welling within him, Rick watched Jack with an eagerness not even six months of careful survival in prison could hide. A key and the information his mother had had a husband before Garrett Thomas—a husband who was, more than likely, his father?

"I'm sorry. From what I've been able to ascertain, since you weren't available, the key was handed over to Garrett Thomas after her death with his assurance that it would be passed directly on to you."

"Garrett was given a key meant for me? Is that legal?" Rick's hand fisted on the desk, but it had nothing on the anger tying his insides in knots. "Why didn't the solicitor hold it for me?"

"He should have. But it seems my predecessor planned to close his practice and hand on all his security packets— estates, legal documents etcetera—to a law firm in Dalton, and he took a short cut. However unwise, it seems your stepfather now holds that key."

"Which means I'll never get whatever it was my mother wanted me to have." The idea of Garrett pawing through papers or discovering who Rick's father was and keeping the knowledge from him left a bitter taste in his mouth.

"We could use legal measures to compel your stepfather to hand over the key. I can set that in motion if you want me to. But setting that aside for a moment, the good news is that he has no legal claim to the house your mother owned. He could have applied to the court for a share of her estate, but he didn't do so within the legal time frame. After this long, there is no possibility of him doing so."

"Does he have any rights to remain in the house, given Harvey is a joint owner with me?" Ownership of his mother's house, even shared with his brother, was a small thing

129

compared to the loss of the key and any chance it might lead him to his father—but it was something. His mother's house meant he had security and a certainty he hadn't been aware of after she passed away. *Security and substance that might make a difference to getting a loan from the bank.*

An errant thought flitted through his mind; why hadn't the house been taken, along with his car after the theft had come to light? But he had no time to ponder.

Jack continued. "You have every right to enter your property, and the right to police assistance, if you think your life is in danger. After your stepfather's threat to use a gun, that assistance shouldn't be a problem."

His right to assistance wasn't the issue; Sergeant Edwards was. But conflict over how to regain the house he'd inherited warred with a perverse pleasure that Garrett could be legally ousted.

"It's enough for the moment to know the law's on my side. When the harvest is in and I've got time to scratch myself, will you do what's required?"

"Absolutely. I'll prepare the documents so they're ready to implement as soon as you're ready to go. But I do advise giving your stepfather fair warning of your intentions, in writing, and including a request for the return of the safety deposit key. I can send that to him tomorrow if you like and set the ball rolling?"

Rick huffed out a heavy breath. The rollercoaster of an evening had been more emotional than he'd expected. He pushed his chair back and stood. "Sure, do that. And thanks for what you've done for me so far. I appreciate it. Er—will you send me a bill for work you've done so far?"

"Now I have a reasonable idea of what is required, I'll do up a costs estimate and agreement. I'll send that via email if you like."

"Thanks. I need a little time to sort out a loan at the bank." Legal costs wouldn't come cheaply, and there would be more work to come after the good news about his mother's Will. He needed to budget. And he needed to speak with the bank manager, although that would have to wait. Everything would have to wait until harvest was over.

Jack glanced past Rick's shoulder, but didn't reply immediately. Rick's skin prickled with foreboding and the urge to turn was strong. He planted his feet and stood straighter. Whatever was coming, he'd deal with it, but . . . Pleasant and professional as the lawyer had been, was he going to request payment in full from his ex-con client?

Jack's gaze snapped back and met Rick's. "Don't worry about part-payment. Settlement can wait until we've got things sorted. I believe you know my aunt, Gloria Sainsbury."

Rick half-turned. Out of the corner of his eye about where Jack's gaze had gone, a six by eight photo of Gloria, her sister, Lily, and Jack with his arms around both women sat on the bookshelf. Jack's connection to one of Rick's *wonderful widows*—his name for the older women for whom he'd done odd jobs before he'd gone to jail—was another surprise. "Gloria is your aunt? Yeah, I know her. Leader of the 'Glam Grannies' brigade of Lark Creek."

"She asked me to say hello and tell you she's waiting for you to—" Jack paused and grinned, a smile full of humour that knocked the lawyer-client relationship on the head. "Hmm, she mentioned something about needing to see your sexy butt up the ladder cleaning out her gutters again. *Her words*. I'm just the messenger." He raised his hands, palms out.

"She wants me to visit?" Stunned, Rick wondered if his fourteen-hour day had led him down a rabbit-hole. Gloria was a stickler for honesty and trust, and he'd been certain his time in prison meant he'd fallen from her good graces. "She does know where I've been for the past six months, doesn't she?"

Jack nodded. "She knows. She also said if you haven't come around to see her by the time the first bottles are laid down at Romney Wines, she'll get on her motorised scooter and come looking for you. Knowing Aunty Gloria, I'd take that as fair warning."

Bemused, Rick promised he'd visit as soon as harvesting was over before thanking Jack again and heading home.

When he pushed open the door to his quarters, a tantalising aroma of lamb curry greeted him. Beside the casserole dish on the scrubbed table, he found a note from Geilis.

You're welcome to eat with me at the house, but if you get home too late, here's dinner. G.

The word rolled around in Rick's mind, gathering the remnants of his sense of self-worth and pulling the shattered pieces of *him* together. Geilis welcomed him. Gloria Sainsbury welcomed him. And Jack Donaldson? His friendly attitude was welcoming too. A small, but growing company of people seemed happy Rick Peyton had returned to town. Even Brett had walked out after their discussion with his head high and his usual slouch nothing but a distant memory. Something had shifted in Rick's world and he felt lighter than he had for many months

I'm welcome, maybe not by everyone, but it's enough.

In spite of everything, was it possible there was a life for him here in Lark Creek after all?

##

Rick's eyes felt gritty as he squinted at his watch. The small figures blurred, but he could see it was past midnight. Three hours sleep wasn't enough. A huge yawn erupted from deep in his belly and he flicked the electric jug on. Coffee, and lots of it, was necessary if he was to be effective on his late night rounds.

Doing night security on top of the demands of overseeing a vineyard approaching harvest left him no time to think, no time to plan how to tackle his stepfather.

Stepfather?

Garrett Thomas was a walking cliché of the worst of that label. But then, he'd not been much of a father to Harvey either, as though Harvey having been afflicted with cerebral palsy was an affront to his manhood. And yet, apparently, Harvey continued to share the house with his father so maybe there was something to Gloria's claim that blood was thicker than water. If that was the case, how would Harvey feel when Rick turned up at their house and claimed his right to live there? Was their shared childhood enough to overcome Rick's increasing absences from home during his teen years?

Closing out all light for several minutes before he stepped out of his quarters, and aided by a thin sliver of moon, Rick pushed aside concerns about Harvey and concentrated on moving quietly. As he passed his gin room, scents of juniper and lemon myrtle teased his nose before he began his evening round. Technically, it was early morning, but he'd tried to vary the times he went out. While his logical brain told him a return visit by the intruder was unlikely, he would continue nightly checks.

Walking past the Romney house on his way back to his quarters, he spied a soft glow through one of the rear windows. Given that Jillian and Reg had left that morning, the light was probably from Geilis' bedroom.

So she can't sleep either?

Was she worried about being in the house alone? His hand reached for the latch on the front gate before he was aware of forming a decision to act. Should he do a sweep around the house yard, or would she be more worried if she heard him outside?

She won't hear me. I'll check it's all fine and leave.

He opened the gate and stepped through beneath the arched trellis. Tendrils of bougainvillea caught his hair before he stepped clear of the archway. Ahead of him, the wide staircase led up to the front veranda, which wrapped around both sides of the house like wings. Below were deep shadows in which an intruder could hide. Keeping his torch low, Rick thumbed the switch on and made a slow sweep of the underbelly of the house. Torchlight illuminated bare earth and dozens of wooden stumps liberally decorated with spider webs. A dark shape scuttled up one of the stumps and disappeared behind a floor joist. If that was the only intruder, they had no problem.

"Rick? What are you doing?" Geilis' sleepy voice made him douse the light and he walked quickly back to the bottom of the stairs. She leaned over the handrail and looked down.

Cursing the mild blindness that followed even the brief use of his torch, Rick couldn't read her expression. He tried to inject some lightness into his reply. "Just scaring away a few spiders as it turns out. I didn't mean to disturb you."

"I wasn't asleep." Her hand rose, pale against the heavy backdrop of an almost-moonless night, and tucked her hair behind her ear. "So, I'm not about to be invaded by an army of arachnids, am I?"

"Pretty sure you're safe from spiders. I was just on my way home. All's quiet at the winery." His vision was adjusting and Geilis was becoming clearer. He was fairly sure she was wearing an oversized T-shirt, but the rest of her body was hidden behind the elaborate curlicues of wrought-ironwork. Both sides of the stairs were delineated by the ghostly metallic patterns.

"Would you like a warm milk or coffee or something?"

"Now?" Her offer caught him off guard and his tired brain struggled to catch up.

"No, tomorrow. What did you think I meant? Of course now."

"Thanks. Coffee would be great."

"I'll put the kettle on. So coffee doesn't keep you awake?" As she led the way up the stairs and into the house, he became aware of a dim glow emanating from the back of the house. As they entered the kitchen, light from the range hood spilled in a soft circle on the cork floor.

"Did you hear me checking?"

"Actually, I was in the kitchen about to make myself a drink and—you'll think I'm crazy, I know. I didn't hear you, at least not consciously—" She set her mobile phone on the bench top and filled the electric kettle.

"Phew, that's a relief. I thought for a moment there I'd lost the ability to move silently."

She gave him a small smile and added a spoonful of coffee to a mug. "I don't know anyone who moves as quietly as you do. But I—sensed a presence outside. I have your number on speed dial and my thumb was hovering over the connect button when I crept onto the veranda, but I could just make out a silhouette behind the torchlight and knew it was you."

"You—knew a vague shape in the dark was me?"

***

Put like that, it sounded worse than it was. Heat crept up Geilis' neck and she turned away, busying herself with pouring milk into a mug and taking her time preparing coffee for Rick. Telling him why she'd know his body anywhere was too embarrassing. It wasn't like she'd been stalking him! But working with him day in and day out, she'd become familiar with the way he moved, the way his lean body bent and stretched, the play of muscles as he went about the more weighty tasks in the vineyard.

And she'd watched him running up the paddock. He moved with lithe grace and power, and—

I might be just a little obsessed with him.

Certain parts of her body tingled at the memory, and she gripped the edge of the bench top. Why had she invited him in for a drink in the dead of night? What was she thinking, indulging in foolish fantasy?

She must be more tired than she thought because here he was in her kitchen in the wee hours of morning. Rick was the distraction she didn't need. Not now, when she was in charge of the winery and the serious work of harvesting lay ahead of them. She didn't need the distraction of Rick—ever.

The microwave buzzer beeped and the electric kettle turned itself off. Thankful for a reason to delay meeting his gaze, she poured hot water on the coffee and stirred it vigorously.

"Are you okay?" His voice sounded concerned, and much closer than the breakfast stool where he'd been sitting. It sounded as though—

"I'm fine. Here's your coffee—" She tapped the spoon on the rim, picked up the mug, turned and took a step—and came nose to top button with his dark shirt. Her heart skittered into overdrive as the heady scent of Rick and his sandalwood soap enveloped her. His hands were by his sides. He didn't touch her; he wasn't crowding her in a corner or making her uncomfortable.

And yet her every sense was focused on him. The surface of the coffee rippled and she gripped the handle of the mug more tightly. Her gaze rose up the tanned column of his throat, over his chin—the stubble was thicker than this morning, and it had looked damned sexy then—and caught on his mouth. Firm lips, currently pressed together; lips she'd be damned if she didn't explore right now.

"Gei?"

Like hot chocolate on a cold winter's night, her name on his lips drew a sigh of longing from her.

He took the mug from her and set it on the bench. At last, she lifted her gaze and met his. Heat hotter than a thousand summer days enveloped her. She rose on tiptoes and brushed her lips across his.

For a handful of heartbeats he remained still, as though caught in suspended animation. She pulled back as far as the bench allowed her. Her gaze fixed on his mouth, afraid to look into his eyes and see how badly she'd misread his interest. Ragged, shallow breaths sounded loud in the silence of the moment, embarrassed by the lack of response from him.

Then he lowered his head and slanted his lips across her mouth. Gentle pressure stopped her wild thoughts, and the slow slick of his tongue teased the seam of her mouth until she allowed him in. She sank into his kiss, sank into the moment when the only thing that mattered was that he didn't stop. She closed the distance between their bodies and still he didn't reach for her. Her fingers touched his hands, bunched into fists at his side.

The past weeks had taught her to recognise the language of his body. His posture said he wanted to act but those tightly furled fingers said action might not be the best choice right here, right now. But she was over waiting. She wanted Rick's touch like she needed her next breath. Sliding her hands up his broad chest, she felt his heart thumping beneath her hand.

"Rick?" Was that husky-voiced woman her? "Look at me."

He opened his eyes. Even in the dim light he couldn't hide from her. Not this time. "Are you sure this is what you want?"

"Totally sure."

He dragged in an audible breath that sounded like the calm before the storm. "If you're sure."

"Rick, shut up and kiss me."

Chapter Eighteen

The alarm buzzed with increasing volume as Geilis rolled over and reached for her phone. White-gold sunlight slid through the gap between the curtains, blindingly bright in her eyes. How could it possibly be morning already? All she wanted was to retreat back into a dream of Rick in her bed. Rick doing incredibly wonderful things that made her body sing. Blindly tapping at the screen until the raucous, high-pitched beeps abruptly ceased, she let the phone drop onto her bedside table and flopped face down into her pillow. Unsure whether she'd hit the snooze or stop button, she groaned.

"Good morning to you too."

That hot chocolate voice, soft, low and addictive, it crashed through the fog of early-morning-too-little-sleep. She flipped onto her back, eyes wide as she looked at Rick. The sheet rubbed across her nipples, sensitive from his attentions in the early hours of morning.

Attentions she hadn't dreamed . . .

He stood, pulling on a pair of boxer shorts over a muscled butt that showed three red fingernail streaks.

Like the cat that got the cream she drank in the sight of him. Pirate stubble and bed hair suited him. Half-naked suited him and inspired her to contemplate starting work late. Holding the sheet across her chest, she sat up. "We don't have to get up yet. Sunrise isn't for a while."

"Sunrise was ten minutes ago. Much as I'd like to stay in bed longer, today of all days—"

The look he sent her spoke volumes and that crazy tingly feeling raced to the sweet, aching spot between her thighs.

"I'll put the coffee on, then swing by my quarters."

"You could stay. It would give us time to—"

A flare of interest lit his eyes, but Rick twitched his shirt off the bedpost and slipped it on. "Work clothes might be a better idea than turning up in black looking like a spy, don't you think?"

Raking fingers through her hair, Geilis tucked it behind her ear and leaned back against the headboard, hugging the sheet tight across her waist. "Do you regret what happened last night?" The possibility it had meant more to her than to him stole the wonder from waking to see Rick in her room. She dragged the sheet higher up her chest.

He sat on the edge of the bed and reached for her. The warmth of his work-roughened hands on her shoulders sent a tingle of anticipation racing through her, and when his lips kissed the sensitive spot below her ear she squeezed her thighs together. No matter what followed she'd never regret last night. But she had to know, even if her pride might be about to take a battering. "Is that what your reluctance is about?"

He nipped her earlobe before lifting his head and locking gazes with her. Flecks of golden morning light seemed to have found a home in his eyes.

"Gei, I don't want what happened between us last night to rebound on you. If I turn up in these clothes it will be clear I didn't spend the night in my own bed. With your parents away, what do you think others will think?"

Really? "You—you're worried about what *other people* think? But it's none of their business."

"It doesn't matter. People gossip. Too close an association with me might not be wise, for many reasons. Your reputation, even the winery's, could be affected."

"Why? You've done your time, now you're employed and you've been entrusted with security. Anyone with half a brain can see the good you're doing here. And everyone knows my father is nobody's fool." She raised her chin and pinned him with a look she hoped carried both her confidence in him, and the challenge she'd thrown down.

"Tell me, in all honesty, didn't you have reservations about hiring me in the first place?"

She raised her chin higher, but couldn't escape the heat filling her cheeks. She hadn't tried very hard to hide her attitude to the ex-con in the beginning; not until she'd promised her father to give Rick a chance. "What if I did? Now I know you, I know better. I trust you, Rick, and so do the people who matter."

"Thanks. You know I appreciate the chance you and your family have given me, but not everyone feels the same. I won't risk your reputation or your business."

"My business is just that—mine."

"And your parents'. Please, Geilis, don't rock the boat on something like this. It isn't worth the possible fallout."

She opened her mouth to refute that, but it seemed Rick was more determined. He dived in, stopping further argument with his lips in a kiss that brought last night rushing back. The memory wrapped her in a cocoon that would carry her through the long day ahead.

The phone alarm buzzed again, growing louder and more insistent while Rick's kiss grew softer until he finally lifted his head.

She opened her eyes. "Fine, I'll let you go now, but tonight—"

"Tonight I'll make a very thorough and very extended inspection of the house, particularly this room. I wouldn't want to see Romney Winery's greatest treasure in danger."

"So—you're going to *personally* guard me?"

"All night long, Geilis. All night long."

Chapter Nineteen

Five days in and the first picking was almost over. Geilis cut a bunch of yellowy-green grapes, small, but packed with intense flavour; what Dad had called 'fruit of the gods' as they discussed the progress of the harvest over the phone. *"I knew you'd be fine overseeing everything, Gei. It's the first harvest I've missed, but these talks with Gervais Armand will give us the edge as we expand our market share."*

And Geilis would be right beside her father for this next step. She breathed deep of the heady smell as the earth gave up her bounty. The vineyard and winery were Dad's passion and his trust in her ability was a precious gift.

One of the quad bikes drove past pulling a stack of filled bins on trolleys attached to the back. She plucked a grape from the bunch in her hand and popped it into her mouth. Early pH and Brix test results were exciting. Now, a burst of intense flavour flooded her tastebuds, adding to her anticipation. As always, her father was spot on picking the date for harvesting this section of white grapes. This was definitely going to be one of their standout vintages.

Gently, almost reverently, she nestled the bunch among the others in an almost-full bin. Across the central path, red grapes, purple-black under the rapidly darkening sky, needed another week or so maturing on the vine. Turning to the almost fully harvested vines of white grapes, she paused for the first time in hours and examined the towering clouds. If they were lucky, they'd finish before the rains hit, but the afternoon heat was oppressive, building like the thunderheads in the eastern sky. Was that a tinge of green near the base of the towering mass of cloud? A knot of worry tightened in her stomach and she set to work with a kind of frenzy. Hail, even pea-sized stuff, was the enemy of a good harvest. Nothing was going to affect their best crop in years, not on her watch.

Rick returned with an empty bin that he set down beside her before picking up the one she'd been filling. "I just checked the BOM. The updated forecast is for twenty millimetres of rain with possible small hail before evening. What do you think are our chances of finishing this section before it hits?"

She focused on weighing the bunch in her hand before snipping it from the vine. "Months of growing and nurturing the vines, and the promise of our best crop in several years, and it could be ruined by a hailstorm. Damn it, we've got to get this section picked and get the netting over that lot of red." A drop of sweat trickled into her eye. Impatiently, she wiped an arm over her face, but didn't change her rhythm.

"Shall I take Grayson and Greg from harvesting to put the nets up?"

"No, they're quick and clean with the shears. Grab Brett and Stacey to help you." She added a final bunch to the bin in Rick's hands and moved onto the next plant.

"I'm on it." He hefted the bin onto the waiting trolley and jumped into the driver's seat. As he drove up the central track, he called for Brett and Stacey to join him.

Geilis didn't stop, but part of her enjoyed having Rick's quiet competence working alongside her. They were a good team; maybe, a great team, like her parents.

"Oh." The random thought knocked her concentration for a split second and she nicked a fat grape globe. Juice dripped onto her fingers.

No. Don't go there.

She wiped the juice off onto her jeans and glared at the grape she'd accidentally cut. *He's not Dad, and we are not a team. Great sex doesn't make us a team.*

But the idea wouldn't budge. Rick wasn't what she'd expected when they'd hired him. Then, he'd been nothing more than an ex-con, a man she'd admired from a distance for his community work—*and for his body, if I'm honest.* His crime, a single mistake as far as she could see, was an aberration. The man she knew was careful and controlled, considerate and intelligent. He could be so much more than he was—a vintner, even, if he chose to follow that path. In spite of the heat, a shiver of anticipation ran down her spine. What would it be like to have him around permanently?

Thunder rumbled, low and distant, and Geilis turned and looked at the cumulonimbus cloud. It reached so high it might touch heaven if such a place existed. A familiar scent wafted past her nose, a scent of rain coming. They had maybe an hour to finish this section before the storm hit.

An hour to harvest and get the covers over the red grapes before the summer storm unleashed its anger against them. She lifted the next bunch of grapes and focused on her vines.

***

The first heavy drops fell on Rick's back as he tightened the ropes holding the netting in place. Geilis had been right about the brothers; they had almost finished picking the last row of white grapes and the trolley had room for their two bins and Gei's last load before he drove it up to the winery.

Brett raised the last pole and called to him. "Ready."

Rick secured the ropes, tested the tension in them, and gave Brett a thumbs-up. "All good. You head on up. I'll drive the quad up when I've got the last of the bins loaded."

"Okay. We'll put the kettle on." Brett and his offsider, Stacey, put on a spurt of speed as they jogged to the workshop. The leading edge of the storm was upon them, but damp clothes were the least of their worries.

Rick headed back to the quad where Grayson and Greg loaded their bins, clipped their shears and grinned at him before they ran up the slope towards the winery. Across the valley, Thornyhill Farm was already veiled in even heavier rain. They needed to get the grapes and themselves inside, now, even if he had to bodily pick up Geilis and hold her to get her to leave any unpicked plants.

He jogged down to the row where he'd last seen her. Frustration and determination warred in her expression, and she grunted as she struggled to carry an overfull bin.

"Here, give me that." He took the bin from her and she bent forward, resting her hands on her knees as she caught her breath, regardless of the rain growing heavier by the minute.

He hefted the last bin onto the trolley, before grabbing her hand. "Come on. Let's get this load under cover."

She nodded and ran back to the quad bike beside him. He jumped into the driver's seat and held out his hand. "There's room for two."

Rain plastered her shirt to her body and she blinked away drops from dark eyelashes as she looked up at him. "Thought you wanted us to stay low-key?"

"Damn low-key. Get up here now. There's hail coming."

She tipped her head to the side. A sharp roaring from the far side of the valley and a thickening blanket of rain were all it took. She stepped up onto the footboard and Rick hauled her across his lap before setting the quad in motion, faster than on previous trips. Getting caught out in a hailstorm with Gei's precious load of grapes wasn't going to happen.

But another part of him enjoyed holding her close in the daylight—close like they had a right to be together. If not for the cargo of grape bins rattling along behind them, he'd pull up in a sheltered spot and pull her around until her legs embraced him—long legs that wrapped around his hips and held him tight in the night. In her bed there was no shame attached to what he'd done, who he was. In her bed, he was just the man who made love to her with passion and tenderness—with the right to be her lover.

It couldn't last.

By the time they passed beneath the metal roller door into the winery, water was streaming off both of them and his clothes felt like they had soaked up a river. He turned off the engine and wiped his face while Geilis took off her hat and beat the water off it. When he looked up, several pairs of curious eyes were watching them. Geilis was draped across his lap looking like a drowned rat. He doubted he looked any better, but the worst thing was the speculative look Stacey shot at them.

Common sense returned and he nudged Gei to get off his lap. He raised his voice for the benefit of their audience. "Sorry about the rough ride, boss."

Frowning, she cast an annoyed look his way, climbed off the quad and turned to look through the open doorway. Not that they needed sight. Heavy rain turned into hail that banged and clattered against the metal roof and sections of galvanised siding on the shed. The noise wrapped around them, making further conversation difficult. Geilis stood very still, watching the tumult outside before she turned and ran an assessing look over the last of the day's picking.

Rick joined her and lifted the first of the bins from the trolley. Raising his voice, he shouted, "That was close, but we did it. Are you okay, boss?"

"I'm fine." She grabbed a bin and wrestled it to the edge of the trolley. When he bent in to lift it, she leaned close until their heads were almost touching. "What the hell is this *boss* business about? Stop it."

"Do you want them to figure out we're sleeping together?"

"What do you mean?"

Out of the corner of his eye, he spotted Stacey and Brett deep in conversation. Stacey glanced their way and smirked before Brett shook his head and pulled away. "Later." He hauled the bin across the concrete floor and set it down at the end of a row of bins of grapes lined up ready to feed the crushing machine.

"Want a hand?" Without waiting for an answer, Brett dropped the far side of the trolley and lifted a bin down. Since giving Brett more responsibility a few days ago, his attitude had undergone a pleasing facelift. Stacey, the other part-timer, was a different matter. Part of Rick recognised that she avoided him wherever possible and he hadn't pushed it. Not everyone was as accepting of his recent past as the Romneys had been.

"Thanks, Brett." It might already be too late, but Rick wouldn't add to the speculation about him and Geilis by behaving any differently than he'd done when he started working for Reg. And if they'd been sprung . . . He'd deal with it in whatever way he could. Protecting Gei and the winery's reputation were the most important things.

More important than being with Geilis?

Squashing the greedy little voice in his head, he hauled bins onto the racks and tried to keep his focus on work. But out of the corner of his eye, he watched as Gei checked the last of the day's harvest before dripping her way into the office.

##

Late that night, after a reheated, slow-cooked meal Geilis had taken from the stash of pre-cooked meals in the freezer, Rick lay beside her. Their lovemaking had been gentle and she'd fallen asleep in his arms on a soft, contented sigh. He trailed his fingers up and down her arm, pausing to circle the soft skin of her inner elbow. She murmured something indecipherable in her sleep and buried her face in his neck. He kissed her temple and held her close.

In her room, in her bed, they were open about what they wanted from each other, giving and taking without reservation. Not hiding their relationship from everyone. But tomorrow or the day after, Geilis' parents would return. Tonight might be his last night with Gei because Rick was certain of one thing. No matter how welcoming Reg and Jillian had been, no one wanted their only daughter sleeping with an ex-con.

Through the open curtains, a rain-washed sky full of stars filled his view. If only the rain could wash away his past as easily as the dust off the landscape. Tired as his body was, his mind couldn't let go of Stacey's smirk and the look she'd given Gei when he'd driven into the shed with her on his lap.

The boss and the ex-con—an item.

What a juicy bit of gossip that would be. With hindsight, he knew Gei straddling his lap hadn't been the smartest move he'd ever made, but damn it all, it had felt good. Every fibre of his being wanted the right to hold her like that—in the sunlight, in full view of everyone, without fear of judgement or the backlash it would inevitably bring to her.

No matter what, he would protect Gei's good name from the taint of association with him, even if that meant leaving Romney Wines. But the thought of not being with her any more left him feeling cold. In his heart he knew he was the man for her.

In the eyes of society—
He'd never be good enough for Geilis Romney.

Chapter Twenty

Wheels crunched along the gravel drive and Geilis took the wooden spoon out of the pot of Bolognese sauce and set it on the draining board. She ran down the front stairs, waving as she jogged along the side of the house until her father pulled into the garage and turned the engine off. Her parents climbed out of their seats and her mother wrapped her in an enthusiastic hug. "Hello, darling."

"Mum, Dad, welcome home!"

"Hello, sweet pea." Her father's hug was warm and welcome. He looked tired and a little greyer in the hair around his face, but happy to be back on home soil. Her stomach reacted predictably, clenching with worry that he'd overdone things on their trip to the city. And yet, the alternative of staying home to oversee the harvest while she attended meetings had been beyond him. If not for strict doctor's orders, her father would have been out there trying to keep up with Rick and the others in a fourteen-hour workday.

And he'd probably have had a relapse. Or another heart attack.

Keeping her voice light, she looked from her mother to her father. "How were your meetings?"

"How was the harvest?" Their questions overlapped and her father smiled. "You first, love." He lifted the boot, leaned in and pulled out his worn black briefcase and the laptop in its purple bag.

"Really good." Geilis handed the briefcase to her mother and helped her father lift the two suitcases from the boot before shouldering the laptop bag and wheeling one of the suitcases ahead of her. "We had the closest run in with that hailstorm, but everyone worked together and we made it—just. Rick drove the last load into the shed and *boom!*—the hail hit."

"Well done. Sounds like you worked well together." He slammed the boot and locked the car with the remote.

Her mother pulled the second case along behind her. "We heard you'd had hail. Your father insisted on leaving Brisbane as soon as our last meeting was over. We stopped overnight in Toowoomba and got an early start this morning."

Her father brought up the rear, having taken the briefcase from her mother. Usually he would have complained his women were making him redundant by grabbing the suitcases. Geilis took that as another sign her father had done too much.

"I see the nets are up over the red sections. I didn't think you'd have time to do that too." He followed Geilis and her mother along the concrete path and up the back stairs into the kitchen. "Something smells good."

"Bolognese, and you should have seen Rick and the others move. He organised them like a military operation. I don't think we've ever raised the nets so quickly and efficiently." She set the suitcase and laptop against the wall before filling the kettle. "I'll bet you'd like a cuppa after that long drive."

"You've got that right, love." Her father lowered himself onto a wooden chair and closed his eyes.

Her mother sat next to him, a hand on his shoulder. "Reg, are you okay? How about you go and lie down. I'll bring the tea in to you."

Geilis watched them, a lump forming in her throat. "Dad? What's wrong?"

His eyelids flickered open and his lips shaped a facsimile of a smile. It didn't fool her. "Just tired, love. Maybe I will grab a catnap before I come over to the office. You can catch me up on everything this afternoon. Unless there's anything urgent . . ."

"Not a thing, Dad. The place is running like clockwork." Geilis dropped a kiss on her father's head and rubbed his back. "I'll bring a cuppa in when it's ready."

He pushed up using the table to steady himself and headed down the hall without another word.

Geilis' mother watched him go before sinking onto the chair he'd vacated. She glanced up, offering a quick smile of reassurance. "He overdid things trying to cram too many meetings into each day so he could be done with it and get back here. I told him you had everything under control—"

Geilis' heart hurt, as though a giant hand squeezed it. All her life she'd believed her father believed in her, in her ability to follow him in the vineyard and crafting top-shelf wines. He'd even told her as much in their phone conversation two nights ago. But he'd wanted to rush back from his meetings because . . . She dragged a breath into lungs that felt tightly constricted. "He didn't trust me to look after the vineyard?"

"Oh no, darling, he trusts you, but he worried that we were leaving you at the worst possible time. If not for needing to meet Gervais Armand, he'd never have left you alone to manage harvest all by yourself."

"I wasn't alone. We have good people working here, Mum, and Rick is—he's really—outstanding."

Her mother nodded. Reaching across the table, she tucked a strand of hair behind Geilis' ear. "So you've changed your mind about him since he first showed up here?" A flicker of amusement lit her eyes, briefly pushing aside concern for her husband.

"I—was too quick to judge. He's proved himself to be Mr Reliable. Honestly, I don't think we'd have got the reds covered in time if not for his organisation. But, Mum, everything went smoothly. We got the harvest in and—You're certain Dad trusts me?"

Her mother patted her hand before she rose to make the tea. "I'm sure. And it's good to hear you're happy working with Rick now because I'm pretty sure your father has plans for that man."

Were plans involving Rick and the vineyard good—or bad? Anything that kept him at the vineyard had to be good as far as work went. Clearly her father wasn't fit enough to take up the reins yet. But as for Geilis Romney—how did she feel about working with Rick indefinitely? Especially since he seemed to be on some misguided path to protect her from gossip. *What gossip?* Who cared who she dated—or slept with? The topic would be academic if Rick didn't want to fall in with whatever plans her father was making.

She shook her head, unable to hold back a soft tut-tut of dissent. "I'll make the tea, Mum. You sit and relax."

Her mother put a hand on her shoulder and gently pushed her back onto a kitchen stool. "Tell me, who needs a seat more—the person who's been sitting all day, or the one who's been hauling bins of grapes?"

"Very little hauling this morning. Besides, I've had a good night's sleep." A very good sleep after Rick had made love to her. She would miss him coming to her bed tonight.

But there's nothing to stop me going to him in the shearers' quarters.

It wasn't that her parents were prudes. They liked Rick; probably approved of his interest in their daughter. But she had to respect Rick's request for discretion. As long as she set her alarm and got back before her parents woke, she'd appease

Rick's desire for secrecy and they could continue to enjoy each other.

Best of both worlds.

Sometime soon though she was going to disabuse him of the silly notion they needed to be discreet. It was nobody's business but theirs. Her reputation wouldn't suffer because she chose to share her bed with Rick. But a small part of her thrilled to the way he wanted to protect her. Old-fashioned as it was, it made a woman feel—

She gasped, reeled, gripped the edge of the bench top. It made her feel— "No, I can't let that happen."

"What was that, darling? What can't happen?"

Her frozen brain came up blank and she blinked stupidly as her mother's smile began to slip. "Uh— Nothing, Mum. I'll be right back." Flashing a quick smile, Geilis walked down the hall and shut her bedroom door behind her. Heart racing as though she'd run a sprint, she leaned back against the door.

Had she allowed herself to fall in love with Rick? Was that what this crazy reaction was? Her bed was neatly made, there were no indents on the pillows, and yet she sensed his presence. Every night for the past eight nights Rick had made love to her there . . .

Her gaze lingered on the queen-sized bed with the apple-green sheets. She closed her eyes and fastened on the memory of him lying there this morning, his arm bent above his head and his face relaxed in sleep. The man she hadn't wanted in her vineyard had drawn from her body the greatest pleasures she'd known. When they were in bed, they were just a man and a woman, but outside—

Rick was right. An ex-con wasn't the most popular employee for a winery aiming at the boutique market. If she loved him, she would want him by her side, and she would proudly proclaim her feelings to the world.

But if she loved him, it could cost her dream.

***

The air was thick with the fruity scent of grape juice as Rick worked alongside Brett, observing and asking questions as they loaded the crushing machine with the first of the grapes. The door to the crushing room opened and Geilis stepped in, Reg following close behind. His usually upright posture had melted and bent like a candle in the sun. Rick glanced around the work space. There were no chairs, not even a stool he could pull up for Reg to perch on.

"How's the crush going?"

Rick wiped his hand on his jeans and offered it to Reg. "Welcome home. It's good, but I'm only here as extra muscle. Brett's teaching me about the process and what to look for. Lots of technical terms, but I'm getting the gist of it." He glanced at Geilis, waiting for her to look his way, to acknowledge his presence, but her gaze was fixed on her father's face, her arm curled around his elbow. Worried, certainly, because close up, Rick could see dark shadows beneath Reg's eyes and a certain pastiness in his skin. Still, she could look at him and give him a smile, but she remained focused on her father, her body curving protectively towards him.

Brett set down the bin he'd emptied into the machine and shook Reg's hand. "The grape quality is high, some of the best I've seen, and the quantity of juice so far is excellent."

"Good to hear. I'm pleased to see you back at your old job. Does this mean things have improved enough at home that you're thinking about coming back full time?"

Brett shrugged, but his expression belied the casual action. "I'd like to, if my sister's condition stays stable. Can I leave it open for another month, until her next specialist visit?"

"Absolutely, Brett. You know you'll always have a place at Romney Wines. Now, Gei and I are going to be in the office for a while if you need us. Rick, can you keep an eye on the tasting room. Tuesdays are usually a bit quieter, but if anyone comes in, you know the drill."

Rick glanced at Brett who grinned. "Don't look at me, mate. I've got crushing to attend to."

"Sure, but wouldn't it be better to have someone serving who knows about the wines, who can talk about them knowledgeably?"

Reg fixed him with a pointed look. "You got a problem telling customers these are the best wines you've ever tasted?"

"No."

"That's easy then. Pour them a taster and let the wine work its magic. Our wines don't need more than that."

"Okay."

At last, Geilis looked up at him from under her lashes, a fleeting look both sexy as all hell and sad. Rick had no idea what to do with it, but there was no chance to take her aside and ask, not with her father holding her arm and Brett nudging him to add another load to the crushing machine.

"Come on, Dad. Let's look at the books." As she and Reg walked away, she cast a single glance over her shoulder. Their gazes connected and held before the door closed behind father and daughter. Rick was left to wonder exactly what had just happened.

Because that last glance looked hellishly like goodbye.

##

Crushing continued while Rick wondered if he'd missed some cue from Geilis. Last night as he held her, he'd thought

157

about asking if she'd come to him in the shearers' quarters. With her parents home and sleeping in the next room, neither he nor Geilis would be comfortable having sex in her bedroom, but the bunks, while offering an intimate space, wouldn't allow a good night's sleep. Not side by side, and Rick wanted Geilis in his arms, curled into his body, head on his shoulder, her breath warm across his chest. Sleeping without her beside him would be cold and lonely.

But—had the time arrived for their brief affair to end? Every part of him rebelled at the idea of not making love to Geilis each night, not waking next to her and watching her sleep, not slipping his arms around her and holding her warm body against his.

It didn't help that he'd known their relationship had an end date; he'd accepted from the start that he wasn't—could never be—her forever man. The reaction from those in town who'd been affected by the theft he'd taken the blame for was unequivocal; his presence could harm the winery in the long term, and he'd never do that to Reg or his family.

If something had happened to make Geilis finally understand what he'd been saying all along, perhaps that was for the best.

The bell on the front door dinged as customers entered the tasting area. Rick grabbed a towel and wiped his hands, tossed his hat onto the table as he walked through the kitchen and took his place behind the tasting counter. "Hi folks, how are you?"

A middle-aged couple in classy, casual clothes hoisted themselves up onto a pair of stools and picked up a set of tasting notes. They had the look of new retirees intent on seeing and doing it all. "Good."

"Passing through Lark Creek, or are you planning to stay overnight?" He set two glasses on the counter and smiled at the woman before taking a sparkling wine and two of the whites from the fridge.

The man gave him a brief, hard look and frowned. "Why is that relevant?"

"We like to know if our guests intend to drive further after they've visited Romney Wines or if they're staying locally. There's an excellent B and B a short drive down River Road, or if you have a van, there's a caravan park about—"

The man held up a hand and Rick stopped mid-sentence. "I get it. Drink responsibly. We'll check out the B and B, but for God's sake start pouring. Heather here's been nagging me to find her a decent winery since we left the Gold Coast a couple of nights ago."

"Dirk, don't be such a pain. I never nag." She turned to Rick and looked him up and down like he was dinner. "I like your thinking, young man. Will you join us?"

Rick shook his head, poured two serves and inserted the stopper. "I never drink on the job."

"That must be hard, surrounded by all these lovely wines." The woman sipped and scrunched her nose. "Oh, I do love champers. The bubbles tickle my nose."

The man tossed down the sparkling in one gulp, set the glass on the counter and leaned towards Rick. "Got any reds, son? The bigger the flavour, the better."

"We have some of the best reds you'll find anywhere. Would you like to try the Merlot, or go straight to our Cabernet Shiraz?" Setting clean glasses in front of the couple, Rick presented the first bottle to Dirk.

"Merlot's for wusses. Pour me a Cabernet."

Heather set her empty glass down and pushed it to one side. "Keep the whites coming for me . . . What's your name, hon?"

"Rick." The bell above the door dinged again. Rick looked at the newcomers and his heart sank. Sergeant Edwards, followed by Constable Brooks, strolled up to the counter, eyed off the couple sipping wine and tucked his thumbs into his belt. "Is Reg around?"

"He's in the office." Rick carefully set the bottle of red on the counter in front of his customers. What was Edwards doing here, and why had he come into the tasting room instead of up to the house? Did it matter? Whatever it was, it spelled trouble for Rick.

Neutral expression, don't give him anything to come back at you with.

"Show us through, will you, Peyton." It wasn't a question. The sly grin as Edwards' gaze held his sent lead weights sinking in his guts.

Rick turned to the couple. "Please excuse me. I'll be back shortly or I'll send someone else to serve you. Follow me, Sergeant." He held the swing door for the police officers, nodded to the customers and let the door swing shut behind him.

On the way to the office, he stuck his head around the door to the cellar. Stacey was counting the newly-delivered barrels and checking them against the list on her clipboard. "Stacey, sorry to ask, but can you look after the couple in the tasting area? They've only tried the sparkling and a Cabernet so far."

Stacey's gaze slid past his shoulder and he guessed Edwards was in view and waiting impatiently. Her eyes widened briefly before meeting his gaze. "Sure." She set her clipboard and pen on top of a stainless steel barrel and strolled towards the steps as Edwards spoke.

"No more delays, Peyton."

Rick knocked on the office door and waited for Reg's "Come in" before he pushed the door open. "The police are here to see you, Reg."

"Tony? To what do I owe the pleasure?" Reg stood and offered his hand. "Have a seat?"

Tony Edwards shook hands, but remained standing. "This is an official visit. We're here to arrest Richard Peyton."

Chapter Twenty-One

Geilis knew the day was going downhill as soon as Sergeant Edwards stepped into the office. Constable Brooks closed the door and stood in front of it, hands clasped loosely at her belt. Handcuffs hung within easy reach and her attention was focused on Rick.

Prickles of unease ran down Geilis' spine like black ants swarming a honey sandwich. Rick stood tall and calm, with a face as expressionless as she'd ever seen. Only his eyes revealed he was worried. That's what mind-blowing sex with Rick had done for her. She doubted anyone else could read his real feelings.

"We're here to arrest Richard Peyton."

The senior officer's words broke through Geilis' musing. "What—why?"

Edwards ignored her. An infuriating smirk tugged at one side of his mouth as his gaze flicked to Rick. Her father sat heavily and Edwards turned to address him. A frown replaced the sergeant's smirk. "Sorry, Reg, but you were wrong about him. He's a wrong 'un through and through."

Clenching his pen in a white-knuckled grip, her father looked from Rick to Edwards. "No, that can't be right. You have the wrong man, Tony."

Edwards shook his head and an expression that might have been pity for her father crossed his face. "I know you want to believe the best of him, but we have it on good authority—"

"What's the charge?" Rick's voice was steady, interrupting Edwards.

162

Distaste created a sneer as the sergeant looked again at the man standing calmly in the background and challenging his authority. "Breaking and entering a building on or around midnight last night. An eyewitness saw you exiting the building and came forward this morning. You were seen and identified, Peyton."

"What building? Who's the eyewitness?"

"We'll go through the details down at the station. Constable—put the handcuffs on him."

Midnight. Last night. When she'd turned into Rick's arms for the second time.

Geilis took a step towards the officer and rested her hand on her father's shoulder. "Wait. Let me be sure I have this right; you're saying Rick broke into some house around midnight last night and stole what—money, household items?"

Constable Brooks hesitated; the cuffs dangled from her fingers, open and waiting to be snapped around Rick's innocent wrists.

Denial thundered in her mind.

Rick stood, arms folded across his chest. Since Edwards' startling announcement, Rick hadn't moved from the spot.

"Stole certain items—yes. We have a search warrant for his quarters and the common areas of the winery. Are you okay with that, Reg?"

"No, I—"

Rick stepped forward. "You're welcome to search my quarters. I've done nothing wrong."

"The cuffs, Brooks. Then Peyton can lead the way to his room. We'll start there."

Slowly, with no sign he was intimidated by Edwards or the handcuffs, Rick held out his hands. Constable Brooks snapped the handcuffs on before opening the door and stepping into the kitchen.

"After you, Mr Peyton."

Once outside, Geilis slipped into step beside Rick on the way to the police car and kept her voice low. "What if someone's planted stuff in your quarters?"

"Then it will be found—without my fingerprints over it, because I haven't taken anything."

"Did you go back to your quarters this morning?"

"No need, after your suggestion that I bring my gear to the house. Damn, sorry, Gei. My black clothes are still in your bedroom. I meant to remove them before your parents came home."

"It's the least of your worries right now." If the stolen goods were found in his quarters—*when they're found*. She was under no illusion—this was a set up, but the *who and why* eluded her. Was Rick correct? Would the lack of his fingerprints on the goods be enough? "They'll say you wore gloves to avoid leaving prints. Rick, tell them where you were last night."

"No, Gei. I won't compromise you. Besides, it won't come to that." His gaze bored into her, willing her to keep her mouth shut, to stay safe from what he saw as the taint of association with him.

The search of his quarters took bare minutes to find a laptop, and cash, stashed beneath a mattress. Constable Brooks proffered the items to Edwards. "These match the details we were given, sergeant."

"Keep looking, Constable. I expect this search could turn up more questionable items."

"Yes, sir." Constable Brooks bagged the evidence, noting where it had been found, before resuming her search.

Sergeant Edwards eyed off Rick. "What do you have to say now, Peyton? Not very smart of you to hide the goods in your quarters."

"I agree it wouldn't be smart, but it wasn't me." Rick looked at ease, if not for the dull glint of handcuffs around his tanned wrists.

"I have an eyewitness who identified you. I'll take his word over yours every day of the week." Edwards hoisted his trousers and hooked his thumbs in his side pockets.

"Who's your witness?"

"A reliable member of the community doing their civic duty."

Geilis hated the know-it-all smirk in the sergeant's voice. She hated the way Rick was automatically *guilty* in the eyes of the law. And she was so over him telling her not to make their relationship public knowledge. She wasn't some wilting flower, unable to handle snide comments that came her way. Damn him, did he want to go back to jail, for a crime he didn't commit? And what would it say about her if she allowed him to be found guilty when a word from her could set everything right?

"Am I a reliable member of the community, Sergeant?"

Edwards' eyes narrowed and he nodded slowly. "I hope so, Ms Romney. Why?"

"Because—"

"No, Geilis." Rick took a step towards her. Brooks laid a restraining hand on his arm, but he halted, his eyes flashing with—was it anger or pain in those dark depths?

She held her hand up, palm facing Rick, locking her gaze on Edwards' assessing face. "This reliable member of the community can tell you with absolute certainty that Rick couldn't possibly have committed a break and enter last night, at midnight or any other part of the night."

The smirk on the sergeant's face disappeared and he took a step towards her. "There's no way you can know that, Ms Romney. Unless—"

"That's right, sergeant. Rick was with me all night. We were in my bed at the house and the only time he moved, I can assure you, I was totally aware of it."

Chapter Twenty-Two

"You'll swear to Peyton's whereabouts under oath?" Sergeant Edwards was definitely angry, but Geilis seemed immune to the waves of official wrath rolling off him.

"Of course. The truth must be made clear so you can catch the real criminals, sergeant."

"Take the cuffs off him, Brooks." A muscle spasmed in Edwards' cheek.

Rick understood how he must have been feeling. Geilis' statement had floored him too, though for different reasons. He held out his manacled wrists, waiting for the click while he watched Geilis stand up to the sergeant. His heart thudded. How long had it been since anyone but his mother had taken his side? How long since someone had proudly announced a connection to him?

The lock snapped open and the metal dropped from his wrists. He'd worn them for less than thirty minutes, but he rubbed his wrists subconsciously, relishing the freedom of movement. But the weight that had been lifted from him was beyond the physical reality of the cuffs.

Geilis had stood up for him. In spite of his attempts to protect her from his bad reputation, she'd chosen to bare the truth about them and hang the consequences. "You didn't have to do that, Gei."

"Tell the truth? I couldn't *not* do it. Besides, I'm rather keen to know who is so desperate to set you up. Aren't you?"

The others paled into the background and it might have been just the two of them in the room for all Rick took notice of anyone else. Her green eyes flashed in passionate defence of him. The wonder of her gift—unexpected and infinitely precious—almost undid Rick. Did she truly believe in him?

The possibility stole his breath before . . .

"Set me up?" He leaned against the wall as the idea sank in.

"Yes."

Why hadn't he seen the pattern earlier? Sensing the attacks weren't about the winery, that they weren't random, he realised he hadn't allowed his deductions to go far enough. This latest incident was proof, at least in his mind, that he'd been right. Coincidences didn't happen. He wasn't just the target. Somebody badly wanted him gone.

Like pieces of the puzzle, he considered the bagged *stolen* items set out neatly on the wooden table. Beside them, the police officer added a small zip lock bag, found tucked behind the tea canister on the shelf above the sink. Small as the quantity of meth was, all by itself it was sufficient to send him back to prison. He tipped his head and considered possibilities.

Who would benefit most from his removal from Lark Creek?

"Is this yours, Mr Peyton?" Constable Brooks lifted the small bag between rubber-gloved fingers.

"No. I've never seen it before." The laptop and cash were common stolen items, but the bag of meth was specific. Someone knew that it would be enough to send him back to jail, should the stolen items fail to do the job. But who was keen—or could that be *desperate enough*—to locate and offer up a bag of meth just to get rid of him?

"You are aware that the conditions of your early release require you to maintain a drug-free record?"

"I'm aware. I don't use, and I've never used. Test me right now. I'm clean and I can guarantee you won't find my prints on either the bag of meth, or the so-called stolen goods."

Sergeant Edwards eyed the bag of meth as it was set beside the other items. He pursed his lips and pinned Rick with a look that was—oddly—missing his usual animosity. "Constable, when you're done recording the items found here, we have work back at the station."

"Am I under arrest, sergeant?"

"No. We'll drop you off at the doc's surgery and get her to take a sample, but, no, you're not under arrest. Not unless that drug test comes back positive. After your test, I'm leaving you in Reg's care. Okay with that, mate?"

***

Geilis' father nodded slowly. "Fine by me." Judging by her father's uncharacteristic frown, he was slowly processing the sergeant's about face.

"I'm not going to leave town, Reg. I can promise you that." Rick's gaze narrowed on Sergeant Edwards. Despite Rick's calm expression, Geilis recognised that tapping of his third finger against his thumb. Her curiosity ran high too. Why had Edwards changed his mind about Rick?

Geilis tried to relax. For now, Rick was free. She gave him a tiny smile, and his gaze flicked to her lips, reminding her of last night. In the spill of moonlight through her window, just so had his gaze claimed her before he'd taken her face between his hands and pulled her down for a kiss, the memory of which melted her insides.

With sudden clarity, she knew last night was not going to be their last together. Recognition of how important Rick had become to her should have made her run a mile. But choosing to announce their relationship to Rick's nemesis was like emerging into the light. Liberating and oh, so right. The world—at least, their small part of it—would soon know she and Rick were lovers.

Edwards frowned and hoisted his trousers. His voice was clipped and gruff as he picked up the evidence bags. "Reckon I know you won't run. Let's go get that blood test sorted."

Relief coursed through Geilis, until she met her father's gaze. His eyebrow lifted, but there was no censure in his hazel eyes.

Warmth ran up her neck and into her cheeks. Was there ever a non-embarrassing way to tell your parents you were sleeping with someone? Not if your name was Geilis Maree Romney. "Ready to go back to the office, Dad?"

He rose from his seat on a lower bunk and shook his head. "I'll get you to drop me off at the house. I think we've got enough to think about for one morning."

Geilis uttered an indecipherable "Mmm" as she followed her father out and opened the door of the ute for him. They peeled away from the police car carrying Rick into town and turned up the home drive, sitting in silence until Geilis pulled up in front of the garage. "I'll just head back up to the winery and—"

"Come inside, Gei. We'll have a coffee and bring your mother up to speed with this morning."

No, no, and no. Chatting with her mother about Rick—especially the part where she had to tell her mother the *testimony* she'd given the police—was the last thing she wanted until she'd had time to sort through the feelings fizzing like fireworks through her veins. "I should really get back and finish—"

"She'll be worrying about seeing Tony's police car here."

"Do you really need me here for that? Can't you tell her, Dad?"

"Wouldn't you prefer to tell her certain parts of it yourself?"

Geilis sighed and took the keys out of the ignition. "Probably."

As they entered the kitchen, her mother set a pot of coffee on the table. "Tell me all about it. I've been anxious since I first saw the police car go past. Was that Rick in the back just now?"

"What did I tell you, Gei?" Her father sank into his corner seat and reached for the coffee pot. "Seems our Rick is being targeted by someone. Gei thinks he's being set up."

As Geilis sat in her usual place at the kitchen table, her gaze fell on the clothes hamper sitting outside the laundry door. Top of the pile of dirty laundry were Rick's black clothes. Closing her eyes, she let her head fall back. There was nothing for it but to tell all.

Her mother's hand squeezed hers. "Do Rick's clothes have anything to do with the police visit, because I know it's none of my business, but—"

"It's fine, Mum. And yes, Rick's been sleeping in my bed since you left, which is just as well because I'm his alibi."

"I'm glad, sweetheart."

Maybe she should have expected her mother's response, but the total acceptance threw her. She turned her coffee mug slowly around between both hands, watching the ripples cross the surface. "That I'm his alibi? I wish he didn't need one."

"Well, if he needs one, I'm glad you can provide it. He's a decent young man. But tell me—" Her mother broke off and took Geilis' hand between both of hers. Geilis met her mother's eyes, so like hers it was like looking into a mirror. They were bright with the hint of moisture in the corners.

"What, Mum?"

"Are you in love with him?"

Chapter Twenty-Three

Through the eastern window, Rick watched a faint brushstroke of colour grow against the pre-dawn sky. *Light winning over darkness*. He turned his head and rested his cheek against Geilis' head. Strands of hair tickled his nose and the scent of her floral shampoo mixed with the scent of sex. He'd give everything he had or would ever be to keep this moment of contentment forever—numb arm and all. He wiggled his fingers, but didn't otherwise move; having Geilis snuggled in beside him was worth every pinprick of pain.

"Are you awake?" Her sultry whisper wafted across his skin.

"Yep. Looking at the sky." He breathed her in, capturing the scent of contentment, fixing these moments in his memory.

"Is the rest of your gin still being delivered today?"

"Tomorrow probably. I'm keen to try Graham's suggestion of adding botanicals to the mix, but I'll wait until the new still is set up. Your dad has given us the whole of today off before we start harvesting the red grapes." Rick trailed a finger along Geilis' bare shoulder towards her collarbone. "A whole day to do nothing if we want."

"Mmm, I know." She nuzzled his earlobe as her foot began a slow journey up his calf. In spite of the fact they'd had early morning sex—the slow kind that bridged dreams and wakefulness—she gave him a heavy-lidded look that almost changed his mind about the day's activities. He needed to speak to Graham but, greedy man that he was, Rick didn't want to let Geilis out of his sight. Or out of touching distance.

He tucked a wayward curl of hair behind her ear. "Would you like—"

"I thought you'd never be ready." In a flash, she pushed him onto his back and sat astride him, and that was the last coherent thought he had until some time later as they lay side by side.

"I must remember not to use that phrase when we're out in public."

"Why not, Mr Peyton? Didn't you enjoy yourself?" She pouted, a pretend pout he nevertheless took advantage of by nipping her lower lip.

"Always, Ms Romney. But I don't want to find myself thrown into a cell for public indecency."

"I'd be right in there alongside you." Sexy tones warmed and invited as her hand tracked down his ribs, heading for points south.

He closed his hand over hers, stopping her move. "You'll be the death of me."

"Ah, but isn't that what the French call it—the little death? I love dying in your arms—over and over and—" She wriggled against his groin, eliciting a groan from him.

"I give up. I'll die in your arms all day, if that's what you want." He dived in for a kiss that gave Geilis no chance to launch another surprise attack. Not that he had anything against her methods, but now it was his turn to pleasure her. He clasped her hips and slid down her body. He was kissing the soft roundness of her belly when her muscles tensed.

She grabbed a fistful of his hair and sat up, pulling him with her. Low-voiced, her gaze was on the closed door. "There's someone outside."

Putting a finger to her lips, he rolled off her, grabbed his jeans from the spare bunk and pulled them on. Picking up the oversized umbrella from beside the door—the most out-of-place item he could imagine in shearers' quarters—he wished it were something more solid, like a cricket bat. Adjusting his grip, he moved quietly to the door, pulled it open and slipped through.

"Man, I hope you're using raincoats for protection in there. That thing won't help." Graham gave Rick a rare grin.

He lowered the umbrella and leaned through the open doorway. "It's fine, Gei. Get dressed and join us when you're ready." He pulled the door closed behind him but the sounds of Geilis getting dressed drifted through. Realisation struck and his eyes narrowed on his friend. "How much did you hear?"

Graham raised his eyebrows. "Enough to know I was pretty sure I didn't want to interrupt you, but there's only so long a man's prepared to listen to you having your fun. Lucky your girlfriend there has good hearing."

"I'm betting you made sure she heard you, unless you're losing your edge, old man?" Rick was certain Geilis would never have heard Graham if he hadn't wanted her to. "I was going to bring Gei up to see you today."

"What for—dinner?"

"Funny man. Actually—" The door opened and Geilis stepped through, one hand self-consciously smoothing her bed hair. The look suited her. It suited him knowing he was responsible for it, and for the glow in her eyes. Tell tale red marks on her neck would corroborate what his friend had heard.

Yesterday, such obvious, intimate signs of their activity would have worried him, but today . . . Their gazes connected and he felt whole, and necessary to her, revelling in the sense of belonging together. Maintaining eye contact because he couldn't look away from her if he tried, he continued. "We were going to ask if you'd seen anything out of the ordinary recently;

anyone coming in here or snooping around the vineyard, weren't we, Gei?"

The smile of a thoroughly well-loved woman tilted her lips and brightened her eyes.

Her gaze clung to his, holding onto their connection and the hazy bubble of their lovemaking until, reluctantly, she turned to Graham. Her smile faded, replaced by a frown as her gaze bounced from him to Graham and back while her mouth formed a soundless O shape.

"Gei?" He reached for her, even as her hand rose to her throat in a most un-Geilis-like gesture.

"I thought you said your father was dead?"

Chapter Twenty-Four

"I'll kill that son of a bitch." Graham's comment exploded and he clenched his hands.

Rick had never seen Graham so lethally angry. He stared at Graham's face, disconcerted to see his own eyes looking back at him, studying him with unnerving intensity. How had he never seen the resemblance between them?

He swallowed years of hurt and pain and anger, and that all-encompassing feeling of not belonging, of never quite fitting in. With single-minded determination, he pushed out the only question he needed answered. "Who? Who are you going to kill, Graham?" If someone was responsible for the lost years between them, he'd be right there at Graham's side doling out justice.

"Garrett—bloody—Thomas." Graham ground out the name, frowned and gave an almost imperceptible shake of his head.

All these years Rick's father had been alive and living within a stone's throw of him. All those wasted miserable years chafing under Garrett Thomas' verbal abuse. And damn it, he wasn't even surprised that his stepfather was yet again responsible for Rick's miserable childhood.

"I thought—he told me—Christ almighty." Graham pulled Rick into a fierce, tight man-hug. Functioning on automatic, Rick's arms closed around Graham. He felt the other man's tension, his hard muscles bunched beneath the khaki shirt as callused fingers scraped his back.

When Graham's hold relaxed, he stepped back with a single sniff and a wipe of his hand under his nose. In all the years Rick had known Graham, this was the closest he'd come to expressing any sort of deep emotion. Graham was self-contained, and Rick suspected he struggled with PTSD, but he'd mastered it to the extent that he'd reached out to a lonely, angry teenager. Neither of them had ever suspected their connection ran deeper than the fact they were both loners, and both felt more at home in the bush than in polite company. Graham huffed out a single hard breath and looked up at the steep sided mountain where Rick had first met him. "All those years . . ."

"How did it happen?" Rick had to know the extent of Garrett's evil, no matter how ragged and scarred it left him.

"I'll leave you two to talk." Geilis dug into her pocket and pulled out an elastic hair tie. A couple of quick movements and her hair was pulled up in a messy bun. She turned to close the door behind her.

"I'd like you to stay, if . . ." Rick looked at Graham. Geilis was the first person he'd felt close to since his mother had passed away. And somehow, it felt right that she should hear his story with him. If not for her observation, he'd probably never have made the connection with his father.

My father. Was this really happening? He breathed deep, seeking to ground himself in the everyday smells and sights. A whiff of cows and dust floated on the breeze from the Henderson dairy, and the high-pitched whine of a chainsaw biting into wood carried from the far side of the valley. Just another workday for everyone else. And the start of a whole new chapter for him.

Geilis stood by his side, rubbing her hand up her bare arm while his father watched him with eyes so like his. How had he missed the similarity all those years? *Because he'd been told his father was dead.*

Graham cleared his throat. His lips pulled up in the semblance of a smile as he looked at Geilis. "Fine with me. Maybe a coffee first?"

Geilis held up a hand and shooed them away. "I'll bring it out in a few minutes. Go on, make a start on your story."

Rick grabbed her hand and pulled her in for a quick kiss. With her free hand, she stroked his stubbled cheek, her touch soft, her eyes full of compassion and wonder. For someone who'd always known her place in the world, known her family and been surrounded by their love, she seemed to get just how momentous this meeting was. He kissed her fingers before she pulled away and left them to talk.

Graham led the way to a patch of shade beneath a small stand of trees, and dropped to the ground, his back against a trunk. "Hold onto her. She's a good one, like your mother."

Rick sat nearby, resting his arms on his knees and looking out across the valley. The solicitor's remarks about his mother's Will and the news that Garrett Thomas was her second husband bounced in his brain, teasing him with his lost history. "Were you and Mum married?"

"Yeah. Too young to be married, her parents said, but that wasn't the only reason. They chucked her out of the family home when she told them she wanted to marry me."

"Mum was kicked out for wanting to get married? Why did they do that?"

A snort exploded from Graham, loud and full of derision. "They belonged to some fancy, schmancy religious group that expected the young ones to marry within their church. Your mother refused, and her parents locked the door on her and sent her packing in just the clothes she stood up in. When you're young and in love you figure you don't need your parents' blessing. We found a marriage celebrant and got married as soon as we could so I was able to access army housing for us. Those months with Laura before I was deployed were the happiest of my life."

Rick risked a glance at Graham's profile. He seemed lost in his memories so Rick waited, giving his friend—*my father*—time to get over the shock. He'd never thought about his mother's life before his birth, or the fact he had no grandparents like other kids. For the first time, he realised how strong his mother must have been to leave her family for the man she loved. Had she thought giving up the only life she'd known for a young soldier was worth the pain of losing her family? "How long did you have together before you were sent overseas?"

"Eight months—not nearly long enough. I was badly injured in a mission that went wrong and ended up a prisoner for several months. I found out later the army told your mother I was missing, presumed dead. I didn't know she was pregnant with you. When I finally escaped, I was taken to a local hospital. About a year later when I made my way home, Laura had disappeared. I even tried visiting her family to see if they'd heard from her. They closed the door in my face. Eventually, with the help of an army buddy, I traced her to Lark Creek. Nearly three years had passed by that time." Graham's mouth clamped shut and a fierce take-no-prisoners hardness narrowed his eyes.

Geilis walked up the slight slope, carrying three mugs in one hand and a packet of biscuits in the other. "I added a slug of rum to the coffee. Thought you might need something more than caffeine."

Rick and Graham leaned forward at the same time to relieve her of the mugs. She looked from one to the other and shook her head. "It's uncanny how alike you two are. I can't believe you never saw it, or that no one in town noticed." She sat facing them and sipped her coffee.

Rick's gaze was drawn to his father's face. Now he knew of their relationship, their similarities seemed obvious, but they'd never stood side by side and looked in a mirror. "Maybe because we've never met in town."

Graham took a biscuit from the packet and dunked it in his mug. "No reason anyone would connect us. I wasn't around when Laura came to Lark Creek, and after I traced her here I seldom came into town. I looked like a wild man in those days—lots of facial fuzz. And I never approached Laura directly. Stayed out of her way. She had a new life and two kids. Why upset the balance when I wasn't in a fit state to help her?"

Suspecting his father understated the effects of his injury and imprisonment, Rick skirted the topic while his mind latched onto simpler, earlier memories. "Mum talked to me about you when I started getting into fights at school."

"Fights? What about?"

"Garrett mostly. By the time I was in grade four, he'd already gone to jail for a couple of minor offences. He was bad news for a kid like me."

"I'd have been worse news back then. I'm sorry, Rick. Horrible as he is, even Garrett Thomas was probably a better option than me. It took me a long time to get my shit together."

Rick's heart ached for the waste; for the lost years and the memories they would never know. In Lark Creek, his mother had put down new roots with his stepfather while his real father had been hiding in plain sight and fighting his own battles. "How long was it before you tracked Mum here?"

"Too long. She thought I was dead and, by the time I traced her here, she'd married Garrett Thomas. When I realised that your mother thought I was dead, I went bush. For a couple of years I lived off the land and virtually saw no one. Then one day I came back to Lark Creek. I'd got myself more together and went around to the house to see her, talk to her. She was out shopping and you were playing in the yard. You must have been five or six at the time."

A faint nebulous memory stirred in Rick's mind. He remembered a tall visitor with long, dark hair in a ponytail, kicking his soccer ball to him—playing with him—before Garrett had come out of the house. After that visit, Garrett had begun his scathing comments. Too young to fully understand, Rick still recalled the change. His mother had become more protective of him. "I think I remember you coming to the house."

"Garrett told me to bugger off and not disturb his wife and children. I had no idea you were my son. He didn't tell me you weren't his." Graham's lip curled in distaste. "Even then he was a dipshit. But I was still a bit of a mess—PTSD they call it now, but at the time I thought anyone was better for your mother than me."

"You were wrong about that. Garrett might not have physically touched Mum, but he's a manipulative son of a—"

Graham's hand shot out and grabbed Rick's shoulder. "How can you be certain he wasn't violent to her?"

"I watched; he became verbally abusive over time, but I never saw him touch her. One day, when I was in my teens, he'd been extra unpleasant and I asked if she wanted me to deal with him. I'd shot up tall and thought I was a man. She told me he'd never physically hurt her, and that she was grateful he'd taken her in when she was desperate and alone with a newborn baby, but I'm sure she never loved him."

Graham's head tipped back against the tree trunk and he closed his eyes for a moment. His hands clenched into fists, and he thumped the ground between them before meeting Rick's gaze. "Much as I want to hate the bastard, he did take Laura and you in when she needed someone. He was there when I couldn't be. But I can't forgive him saying you were his son. He's denied us both a lifetime of knowing one another. If only I'd talked to Laura."

Seeing Garrett through Graham's perspective unsettled Rick. For too many years, his stepfather had been the villain with nothing to redeem him. A debt of such magnitude and the idea that Garrett had had a shred of decency at one time by taking in Rick and his mother would need some serious mental adjustment. "If he could do that, I wonder what changed him into the arse he is today?"

A twisted sort of logic punctuated Graham's terse explanation, but Rick struggled to understand how his father could have left his wife in another man's care. Damaged as he was, surely if he loved her . . .

Graham's mouth clamped shut and a muscle jumped in his cheek.

He wasn't the only one finding this talk of the past tough. *For God's sake this was his mother Graham was so casually dismissing as a problem he couldn't manage.* Aware of his hands clenching, Rick flattened them against his thighs. "I don't buy it. Damn it, you said you were so in love, she left her family for you. How does that disappear?"

"It doesn't. I loved your mother then, and I will to my grave." He dragged in a deep breath, exhaling slowly. Shaking his head, he met Rick's angry gaze. "I doubt what I did makes sense to you. Back then, it was the only thing I could do. I kept an eye on your mother through all those years."

Before Rick's brain framed the thought, Geilis jumped into the conversation. "But your PTSD—you could have got help. Surely the army would have dealt kindly with you?"

"Maybe. I don't know . . ." He took a long drink of his coffee before setting the mug carefully on the ground. "I wanted her to remember the man I had been, not the shell I'd become. I'll go to my grave regretting that I had nothing left inside to give to her."

"Under the law, you might have a claim to Mum's house. I never thought about where she got the money for it, but maybe your pay went to her while you were missing. Do you think the army gave her a pension or something?"

"It's probable. As for her house—that should belong to her children. Besides, what would I do with a house? I can't bear to be inside four walls."

"Claustrophobia?" A shudder ran down Rick's spine. He understood the fear all too well; he quirked an eyebrow in unspoken query.

"Prison does the same to some men. Me? I need air and space and the longer the view, the better." Graham nodded and rose lithely to his feet.

"I should head off."

Rick stood and offered Geilis his hand and pulled her to her feet. "What did you come down off your mountain for? You never got around to telling me and I'm damned certain it wasn't to share the family history."

Momentarily diverted, his father took a small plastic packet from his pocket and handed it to Rick. "Sim card. Night exposures, but clear enough to take to the police. Garrett's responsible for what's been happening here—the pipe, although I can only testify to what I saw from up there." He jerked his thumb back towards O'Reilly's Ridge. "After I spotted that little bit of devilry, I set up regular surveillance. I see a helluva lot from the ridge, and Reg has been good to me. I pulled out the zoom lens and the SLR camera. The vandalism and the stuff planted in your room is documented on the card."

"How—why did you—?"

"I've been coming down at night and keeping a watch on the place too. Good move, by the way, changing the time you do your rounds. You almost caught me the other night." He clapped a hand on Rick's shoulder and squeezed. "Take that to Edwards and tell him where you got it. Edwards isn't the sharpest tool in the shed but he's not corrupt."

"Thanks, Gra . . ." The rest of the word stuck in Rick's throat. For all that he had used that name for the past seventeen years, it was wrong. He swallowed and met the eyes of the man in front of him. "Thanks, Dad."

Chapter Twenty-Five

Geilis twined her fingers with Rick's as they walked up the path and stopped at the bottom of the steps that led into the Lark Creek Police Station. A curious high coursed through her body after the rollercoaster morning of revelations, but above all she felt relief for Rick. Knowing who you were, where you came from—things she'd taken for granted—they meant more than she'd understood before he'd come into her life.

"I like your father. He's a good man. To think he did all that surveillance for us—for you."

"For you and your family, Gei. He didn't know me in any way that mattered to the vineyard. He did what he saw was right."

"I'm beginning to understand that about him. It's almost like he's trying to make up for not being there for your mum by looking out for Lark Creek." Geilis put her foot on the lowest of three steps. "Shall we go in?"

Rick didn't follow. A muscle jumped in his tight jaw and he stared at the door as though it led into a narrow, confined cell rather than the high-ceilinged, open plan office visible through the glass.

A frown wrinkled his forehead as he turned to her. "Why don't you hand over the Sim card? It's your winery that my stepfather targeted."

"Stop getting so hung up on the '*my stepfather*' thing. Your *father* provided the evidence. That's what you should be focusing on. It's appropriate that his son be the one to hand it over. Like father, like son." Didn't Rick realise he was a good man, too? He'd stolen—yes—but everything she knew of him shouted that was an aberration, an act at odds with the man standing beside her now. It wasn't who he was.

Rick was decent and honest, and her heart was saying he was the man for her. The idea was less scary than when he'd driven the quad bike through her vineyard that first morning. A flicker of embarrassment licked through her. No matter how long ago it seemed, she couldn't get past the fact she'd judged him and found him wanting. Just like others in town who didn't know him well.

She met his gaze and nodded towards the door of the police station. "Are you coming in?"

His hold on her fingers tightened as his gaze flicked from the glass-panelled door to the window and peered into the interior. His Adam's apple bobbed up and down, and his closed expression reminded her of Graham Muggeridge revealing his claustrophobia. Was that why Rick hesitated? Did he share the same gut-wrenching fear as his father, or was this about his self-image as a convicted thief? "Rick? Is this about confined spaces or are you worried what the police will think when you walk in there?"

"I'm an ex-con handing in evidence against another criminal. How do you think I feel?"

"You're a citizen of Lark Creek doing your civic duty, a man intent on doing the right thing."

He turned his head and his dark eyes seemed to reach inside her, searching for something important. Truth. Her truth.

"Is that honestly how you see me, Gei?"

"First and foremost, I trust you. And you're the man I chose to sleep with because I trust you."

The ghost of a smile tugged at the corner of his mouth. "I thought it was because of my muscles. Isn't that why you reluctantly agreed to hire me?"

Geilis tapped her chin and pretended to consider his question. Keeping it light had eased the strained look around

Rick's eyes and mouth. Later, she planned on taking his mind off everything except their bodies, and all the delicious ways they could play together. But in the meantime . . . She looked up at him with a flirty look. "Hmm, well there is that bonus. I mean—your *muscles* are very appealing."

"Good to know. Maybe later you can tell me which of my muscles is your favourite." As he turned towards the front door of the station, tension leached back into his body.

"What your stepfather has done is nothing to do with you."

"Part of me knows that, only—" He huffed out a short, explosive breath and raised his chin. "You're right. Thanks."

Squeezing his hand, she gave him a smile. "Let's do this. Then I'll shout you lunch at Bailey's hotel."

"Lunch, right. It's our day off." She waited for Rick to make the first move and together they climbed the three steps and entered the police station.

***

Rick let go of Gei's hand and placed the Sim card on the counter as Constable Brooks approached. "Good morning. We have evidence about the criminal activity directed at Romney Winery, and further proof of the identity of the person who planted the items found in my quarters." The cells were through a nondescript doorway in the back-left corner. Rick swallowed and kept his focus on the officer.

Marion Brooks looked at the plastic case beneath his fingers before meeting his eyes. "Photos? Who provided them?"

Rick wanted to say it was his father, but respecting Graham's privacy had been second nature to him for more than half his life. He pushed the case across the counter top with one finger. They'd made a copy for his peace of mind, but still the act of handing over evidence felt—strange. "Graham

Muggeridge brought this in to us this morning. We had no idea he was keeping an eye on the vineyard."

"The hermit up on O'Reilly's Ridge? I thought he was a myth."

"No, ma'am. He's flesh and blood, but he doesn't like crowds or towns." Or being inside a building. Father and son shared an aversion to four walls. And his father's attitude to Garrett Thomas, complicated as it was by an odd mix of gratitude and dislike, probably wouldn't make sense to the police, even if Graham could be brought to explain his past. "He handed that card to us and asked us to bring it in for him."

Gei leaned on the counter beside him. "You should get Graham's statement about the damage to the watering system too. He mentioned he'd seen what happened, and that led him to keep watch with his camera."

Sergeant Edwards ambled up and joined the constable behind the counter. Rick had been so focused on passing on Graham's message he'd momentarily forgotten his surroundings. The familiar tightening in his belly rose up his gullet and strangled his next breath. He coughed to cover any tell-tale signs of discomfort.

"So you're telling us that this Sim card is from Graham Muggeridge?"

"That's correct, Sergeant." Geilis was quick to jump in.

Had she noticed how Rick tensed when Edwards came near? And yet he had to hand it to the sergeant; since the failed attempt to have Rick's parole withdrawn courtesy of the planted drugs and stolen goods, Edwards had reined in his natural sarcasm and was all business. If that was the new norm, it would take some getting used to.

Edwards held out his hand and Brooks dropped the card case into his meaty palm. "We'll review this and add it to the file, Ms Romney. Brooks, note the details and join me in my office. I want to see what Graham's caught on camera. Can you wait while we review it?"

Wait . . . Could he wait here? The walls of the station towered over Rick, quivering and bending in as though they would crush him beneath the weight of the building. His lungs tried to pump but there wasn't enough air in the room. Inside his head, his brain shrieked a warning.

"We'll stay in town." Needing to get outside, Rick turned. It took all his self-discipline to stand and hold the door for Geilis.

Geilis took two steps towards the door and turned back to the police officers. "We're heading up to Bailey's hotel for lunch if you have any questions after you've looked at what's on the card." She nodded and then preceded Rick through the door.

Once on the footpath, Rick drew in a deep breath and tipped his head back. Nothing but blue sky filled his vision. Maybe it was that newfound sense of freedom, or more likely it was Gei's belief in him, but Rick slung an arm over her shoulders and kissed her temple—in public. "Thanks for that."

"What? Standing there like a statue?"

"Reminding me I'm more than a jailbird on parole. I've been living under the shadow of what I've—" The rest of the sentence choked him. Not what he'd done, but what he'd chosen to do after the fact. For the rest of his life he'd have to live with that choice, and its consequences, but he'd be damned if it defined who he was.

Gei stepped in front of him and her hands held his face, her green eyes pinning him with that don't-dare-say-a-word-until-I've-finished look. He kept his mouth shut and drank in the sight of the woman who had opened the door of his self-imposed isolation.

"Rick, I never ever want to hear you talk like that again. Starting today, right here, right now. What's done is in the past. Now, you have only to choose whether you want to go forward or retreat behind your defensive wall. Even Sergeant Edwards is coming around. Don't let—" The rest of her pep talk vanished as his brother, Harvey, clomped to a stop beside him.

"Rick. I'm glad to see you at last. Why haven't you been around to the house?"

Chapter Twenty-Six

"Harvey, what are you doing in town?" His half-brother leaned on the pair of forearm crutches that had been part of his life since his battle with meningitis had left him with a rare form of cerebral palsy. Instantly alert, Rick looked around for Garrett. "Did your father drive you in?"

"Yeah. He did, but I said I'd meet him at the post office in fifteen minutes." Harvey eyed off Geilis and smiled. "I'm Harvey, Rick's brother."

"Hi. How come I haven't met you before?"

"Weird, hey? Lark Creek isn't exactly a metropolis." Harvey shrugged. "But then I don't get out much either."

Hoping he wasn't being rude but concerned that he'd come face to face with Garrett, Rick scanned both sides of the main street and as far down Leonard Street as he could see. Reluctantly he brought his attention back to the two people who meant the most to him. Recalling this morning, he amended his thinking.

Two of the three most important people in the world.

"Harvey, this is Geilis Romney from the winery. Harvey was home schooled by our mother, so you wouldn't have seen him at school." Because he'd been fragile and damaged, and his mother had blamed herself for her youngest son's health problems. Rick looked up and down the street again. How independent was Harvey these days?

There was no sign of Garrett along the street, but the evidence Rick and Gei had just handed to the police would probably put his stepfather back in prison for a reasonable term. A boulder lodged in Rick's throat. What would Harvey do without his father? Garrett going to prison would isolate his brother even more now their mother was gone. He zoned back into the conversation.

"Mum worried about me getting hurt at school. I've got cerebral palsy." Harvey raised one of his forearm crutches as though Geilis might have missed seeing them and turned back to Rick. "So, why haven't you visited since you came home?"

Geilis touched Rick's arm. "I'll leave you and your brother to catch up and meet you at home later?"

God help him, Rick needed to talk with Harvey and get him ready for the changes that were coming, but not here, in the middle of town. Prying eyes saw everything, and he didn't want the case against Garrett failing because he spoke out of turn. Shaking his head, he slipped an arm around Gei's waist and pulled her close. "Trying to get out of buying me lunch, are you?"

"Absolutely not, but I thought you two might like a few minutes alone. How about I go on up to the hotel and get us a table? You can wander up when you're ready."

"Good idea."

She held out a hand to Harvey. "Lovely to meet you. I hope I'll see you again soon." With a smile and a quick kiss on Rick's cheek, Geilis strolled off in the direction of the hotel.

"Okay, so I can see why my brother hasn't bothered coming to see me." Harvey lifted one arm and nudged Rick. "You've had your hands full I guess."

"Geilis isn't the reason, Harvey. I wanted to see you, but Garrett—he wasn't welcoming. It was safer—better for me to stay away."

"What do you mean, *safer*?"

"Look, do you mind if we talk about this later. I promise I'll come to the house, just not when Garrett's there. Okay?"

"I get that you and Dad don't get along, but he's not a bad man."

Unable to agree, Rick put a hand on his brother's arm. "Hey, have you finished developing that online game since I was last at home?"

"Yeah, and I'm about to talk to a guy who knows someone at one of the big game creators. He reckons they'll kill to get their hands on it."

"Great, Harv. Maybe you can show it to me when I come over, although I doubt I'll be much good playing it."

"I can teach you, Rick. It's just you haven't spent as much time on computers as me."

Yeah. Rick Peyton and computers were opposite sides of the knowledge fence. Funny no one questioned his lack of skill when they charged him.

"If you're going to meet your dad you should probably head up to the post office now. I'll come by to see you—soon."

He watched Harvey heading along the footpath with his oddly agile swinging gait before turning away and heading for the hotel and Gei.

***

Eavesdropping.

Geilis' parents had taught her no good ever came of it and her natural inclination had been to keep walking along the corridor towards the ladies restroom, but the way Garrett Thomas had spoken Rick's name—as though he hated and despised his stepson—caught her attention. It would have been so easy to assume Garrett's attitude came out of Rick's jail sentence if Garrett himself hadn't served time.

Geilis shook her head. It didn't make sense, but she flattened herself against the VJ wall beside the open doorway, all but holding her breath. Scruples be damned. If Garrett was talking about Rick, she wanted to know more. First checking the hallway was clear in both directions, she peeked around the edge of the doorway.

Garrett sniggered as he set his half-empty schooner on the bar and leaned towards his drinking partner. "Thinks hisself so smart but he had no idea I'd hacked the computer. Set him up tight as a drum and made a tidy sum for meself."

"Never knew you was a computer whiz." Wobbly Wilson snorted and raised his glass in a mock toast to Garrett.

"I wasn't until last time I was nicked. Got meself a cell mate who knew his way around computer security. Helped him a time or two. He showed me a few tricks in return for looking after him."

"How did you help him?"

"He was a pretty boy. 'Nuff said."

"You mean . . ."

"Yeah. If I didn't want him stinking up our cell, I had to keep an eye out while he showered. Pity the poor bugger who's in with him now if they don't do the same. What horse ya got in the two-thirty at Flemington?"

Geilis' blood ran cold. She leaned against the corridor wall and stared at a faded nineteenth century political cartoon without seeing any humour in it.

Rick went to jail and he's innocent. His stepfather set him up.

Geilis pushed off the wall and tottered on legs that wobbled like overcooked spaghetti on to the pub veranda. She gulped in a lungful of air heavy with the stink of stale beer and blood and bone from the garden below. Hard evidence might be missing from her certainty, but she'd stake everything she had, including the vineyard, on her belief in Rick.

He had quietly gone about helping seniors in their community and refusing payment in between his regular work, seeing to the little jobs around their homes that were beyond their physical abilities, so they could stay in their homes as long as possible. Embezzling money from his work place had made no sense to her, and yet . . . The police had found evidence of his so-called guilt in a new bank account in his name, in transfers made—from Rick's family's computer.

The only possibility Geilis had come up with was that someone had set him up, but that meant someone living in Rick's home. And now her suspicions had been confirmed out of Garrett's own mouth.

Why didn't Rick fight it? Why would he do jail time when he was innocent?

Damn it, he could be heading into the hotel right now. If he came face to face with his stepfather after this morning's news, it wouldn't go well.

Geilis thumped the railing and ran down the side steps. She needed to head Rick off.

***

Geilis jogged around the corner, all but crashing into Rick. One hand slapped against his chest and pushed him back from the corner. He took hold of her shoulders and waited for her to smile. Beneath her tan her cheeks were flushed, and the expression in her eyes was unreadable. Green and hazel flecks fought for dominance as she met his gaze. Was she angry or worried?

"Geilis, what's wrong? Are you okay?"

She started to shake her head, glared at him, and then, while he was trying to recall if he'd done something to upset her, she cupped his face in both hands and kissed him.

His hands settled on her hips while his tongue sought her parted lips. Passion and urgency zinged in the kiss and part of his mind wondered if the electricity they generated was visible, crackling in the air around them.

Abruptly she pulled away. "You're an idiot, Rick Peyton. A bloody idiot."

"Make a habit of going around kissing men then telling them they're stupid, do you?" Bemused, he folded his arms and leaned against the shop front.

"How could you not know . . ." Her breasts rose as she drew in a deep, slow breath and expelled it in a rush.

"There's a lot I don't know. Which fact in particular is this about?"

"Your stepfather. He set you up."

Rick took a step towards Geilis and planted his feet. Mention of *set up* linked with Garrett's name sent adrenaline racing through his veins and squeezed the air from his lungs. Why had she mentioned the one person guaranteed to spark his anger? Discussion about his stepfather had dominated their morning and Rick sure as hell wasn't going to let him ruin the rest of the day. He had plans, which involved Geilis and a bed and little else.

But Gei thumped his arm and poked him in the chest. "Did you hear me?"

"I heard. What makes you think he set me up?"

"I overheard him talking to Wobbly Wilson at the pub. Garrett told Wobbly he'd hacked your account. His exact words were he'd '*set you up tight as a drum*'.

"He doesn't have the skills. Even my pathetic tech skills were better than his. Empty boasts, Gei, that's all it could be." Disappointment filled Rick's brain like black fog.

If only – if only –

"Rick, listen to me, his last cell mate was some sort of tech whiz hacker who traded the 'how to' secrets in exchange for protection from Garrett."

"*Garrett* hacked the company accounts and set me up? Shit. I thought it was Harvey."

Chapter Twenty-Seven

Rick grimaced and corrected the car's angle as the vineyard ute bounced out of a pothole. Ahead of them, the police wagon turned onto twin dirt tracks that led to a small Queenslander—his mother's home. The wailing siren diminished and cut out as the vehicle drew to a stop on the driveway. Sergeant Edwards had agreed to allow Rick to follow them out to the house to be with his half-brother when they arrested Garrett, on the understanding Rick remained at a distance.

Rick pulled up behind the police vehicle as Edwards and Brooks climbed out of their car. Edwards hoisted up his trousers and checked the clip on his gun holster. Rick turned off his engine, removed the key and looked at Geilis. "This is a bad idea. I don't know how Harvey will cope home alone. I don't think he's fully independent."

"What is this? Are you seriously questioning whether arresting your stepfather shouldn't happen because he looks after Harvey? Honestly, Rick—"

"Of course not. But this isn't the homecoming I'd wish for."

Rick got out of the ute and crossed the dirt tracks to the front steps as Harvey appeared on the veranda and leaned over the railing. "Rick, why are the police here? What's going on?"

Rick stopped and looked up at his brother. "Harv, I'm sorry, mate. Where's your father?"

"Down at the shed. But Rick, the police?"

Constable Brooks joined Rick and looked up, compassion filling her clear gaze. "Mr Harvey Peyton?" When Harvey nodded, she held up two pieces of paper. "We have a search warrant for these buildings and a warrant for the arrest of your father. Where is he?"

"Like I told Rick, he's in his shed. But—what are you arresting him for?"

"Thank you. We'll be back with your father in custody. Please remain in the house with your brother." Brooks strode off down the driveway.

Minutes later, the voices of the police officers demanding admittance could be heard across the paddock separating the house yard from Garrett's shed. For as long as Rick could remember, the shed had been out of bounds. He'd loathed Garrett enough that he'd never wanted to go near the place. If his stepfather chose to remove himself and leave his family in peace, Rick didn't care why. He walked slowly up the steps. "Want a coffee or a beer? They might be a while."

Harvey planted himself in front of the doorway and glared at Rick. "Tell me what's going on. I'm not a baby, Rick. I don't need you to wrap me in cotton wool. I can handle whatever it is."

Rick sensed Geilis behind him before the subtle hint of sage and lemon body wash gave her presence away.

"He really does deserve to know, no matter how difficult it is to tell him."

"I know. Can we at least get a drink first?"

"Fine. Drink, then details." Harvey led the way down the dark hall to the kitchen. He yanked the door of the fridge open and tossed a can to Rick. Looking at Geilis, his anger dissipated. "Would you prefer coffee?"

"A beer is fine." Geilis slipped past Rick and put a hand on Harvey's arm as she accepted the can. "Thanks. I'll just go out and look at the view if you two—"

"Gei, it's okay. You know as much as I do. Tell me if I leave out anything important." Rick led the way through the back door, holding the mesh screen wide as the other two joined him. The narrow back veranda looked west over bleached-blond grass paddocks towards a distant line of trees that marked the course of Lark Creek. Off to the right, beyond a line of barbed wire fencing and a cattle grid they'd never needed, Garrett's shed hunched behind a line of trees that almost shielded it from view.

Rick leaned on the railing and took a swig of beer from the can. "What does Garrett do in his shed?"

"I've no idea. Is it relevant to what's happening?"

"Probably not. Okay, so—have you heard about recent incidents at the winery?"

Harvey frowned. "My friend Jonah told me there'd been a break in. His sister works there."

Gei nodded. "That's Stacey. Jonah helped with the harvest one year before he went away to university."

"Yeah. Harvest sounded pretty cool. So? How is what happened at the winery connected to Dad." Harvey clutched the can and looked expectantly at Rick.

There was no easy way to do this. "Evidence was given to the police identifying Garrett as the person responsible for the break in."

"Why would he—no, it can't be true." Colour faded from his brother's face, highlighting shadows beneath eyes as blue as their mother's.

Geilis set her can down and put a hand on Harvey's arm. He turned a troubled face towards her.

"It's true, Harvey. Garrett damaged a barrel of wine, but worse than that, he attacked Rick. See that scar on your brother's temple? A crowbar thrown by your father caused that. I'm sorry."

Harvey's throat rippled and his head shook in small side-to-side shakes. Rick wondered if they were in response to the current stress. "Shit. It sounds serious."

"Yeah, sorry, little bro. Garrett's likely to go to prison again. But if you can stand to have me around, I'll move back home. You know, help out around the place. Only if you want me to." Harvey's brow furrowed, and Rick waited on his answer, surprised by the surge of longing to reconnect with his brother.

"That would be cool, Rick. I'd like that."

Rick expelled the breath he hadn't realised he'd been holding. "Great. I'll see about moving my gear toni—"

An explosive *boom* rocked him back on his heels and his gaze fixed on Garrett's shed. A ball of flame and black smoke shot twice as high as the trees and a dull roaring filled the air.

Rick called over his shoulder as he raced for the stairs. "Call an ambulance and the police from wherever's closest. Tell them there's been an explosion and an arrest that's gone wrong."

Chapter Twenty-Eight

The sirens faded into the distance as the ambulance carried both police officers with minor injuries to the Dalton hospital, while the rescue helicopter flew Garrett Thomas to the Toowoomba Base Hospital. Through the kitchen window, Geilis watched the airborne dot disappear over the hill before picking up her tray and carrying it to where the two brothers sat side-by-side on the back veranda. "You did an amazing job getting Garrett out of that fire, Rick."

Geilis handed each of them a mug of coffee, wondering if she'd missed her calling in life. Twice in one day as a barista probably didn't qualify her to switch occupations. Rick turned his soot-covered face, looked up at her and raised an eyebrow in an unspoken question.

Geilis nodded. "Yes, it's got a double shot in it."

"Thanks."

As he raised the mug to his mouth, she noticed blood streaking the back of his left hand. "Let me see that. Does it hurt?"

Rick glanced down, switched the mug of coffee to his right hand and flexed his left. "It's fine. I don't think it's mine. Probably—" His gaze flicked to Harvey, sitting nursing his mug and looking more than a little shell-shocked.

"Right. Maybe you should clean it off before the police interview us."

He nodded and sipped his coffee before setting the mug on the weathered table and pushing to his feet. "Back in a minute, Harv. Okay?"

Unsure what to make of Harvey's lack of interaction, Geilis wrapped both hands around the mug and sipped her coffee. Her gaze snagged on the black smoke that spiralled up lazily from the charred remains of Garrett's shed, and the white coveralls of forensic police as they moved around the crime scene. Black and yellow tape flapped across the nearby cattle grid.

"Dad was operating a meth lab, wasn't he?" She'd expected Harvey's first words since the explosion to express concern for his father, critically injured as he tried to destroy evidence of his activity. But there was no surprise in Harvey's question, just a statement of fact.

"Apparently so."

"How could I have lived with him here all this time and never known what he was doing? How is that possible?" Blue eyes beseeched her for an answer. She had none to give.

"Maybe, in spite of everything, he wanted to keep you out of what he was doing. It seems he was very good at hiding his activities—the shed was so far from the house, and there aren't any neighbours nearby to complain about the smell."

"I lost my sense of smell years ago. Dad knew that. I'll bet Rick would have smelled it." Harvey looked up suddenly, wide eyes fixed on Geilis' face.

"What is it, Harvey?"

"That's why Dad didn't want Rick anywhere near the house. Rick would have known straight away what was happening and gone to the police."

Movement behind her gave away Rick's presence before his hand settled on her shoulder. "Harvey thinks he knows—"

"I heard. You're right, kiddo. Garrett had to keep me away from here at all costs. You have to give it to him. Getting me busted for breaking my parole conditions shows a certain twisted logic." With a quick squeeze of her shoulder, Rick moved past and sat beside his brother. Leaning forward, he clasped his hands between his knees. "I'm sorry my coming back to Lark Creek means you've lost your father for the foreseeable future."

"Don't be sorry. He's committed crimes and hurt you and he has to pay for that, but Dad was never unkind to me. Not like he was to you. With my health problems and not driving and all that, maybe he didn't see me as a challenge."

Geilis suspected anger caused the glitter in Rick's eyes, but his tone was gentle. "Then he was wrong about you. You've got a brilliant mind and that game of yours—it's going to do really well."

"I hope so. You can try it out with me when you move in."

Rick grinned and ruffled his brother's hair. "You might need to teach me how to use the computer properly so I can play it with you."

A thought niggled in Geilis' mind, an idea so strange she thought twice before broaching it. "Do you seriously not know how to use a computer? In this day and age, that's got to be some kind of record."

Rick shrugged. "I'm pretty basic in what I can manage to do online. It's never interested me like it does Harvey. He's the whiz kid in technology. He left me eating his techno dust by the time he was eight."

"Right, so— I get that you thought you were protecting Harvey by accepting blame for the theft, but explain to me please, how is it possible that *anyone* believed you were the mastermind behind a crime involving hacking a computer?" She glared at Rick.

Two men, brothers, turned to her. Sired by different men, they didn't look as dissimilar as she'd first thought. Blue eyes and dark brown eyes looked at her and their similar expressions revealed their innate honesty and humanity. Given that Garrett Thomas had loomed large in the childhoods of both, that made the type of adults they'd become even more remarkable.

Harvey chuckled, his laugh growing, expanding, taking over the quiet afternoon until he fell back against the chair. "Him—a hacker!" He pointed at his brother, spluttered, and collapsed again in a quivering mass of good humour.

Slowly, Rick's lips curved up in a smile that ignited a slow burn in Geilis. Her gaze narrowed on him, on the promise in his wickedly tempting grin. They'd had very different plans when they'd woken this morning. And this day wasn't over. Not by a long shot. He leaned forward and rested his hand on her knee. His touch fanned the slow burn of his smile into flames every bit as hot as those that had rolled off the meth lab.

Rick was her drug of choice. She touched her tongue to the corner of her mouth, feeling good, feeling powerful when his gaze followed the movement.

His hand slipped a little higher up her leg and she pressed her thighs together. Not fair, not here where she couldn't act on the rush of lust. Damn him, he knew what he was doing to her.

"Maybe I'm a better actor than I am a winemaker."

Clapping a hand over his, Gei slid her free hand up his thigh, not high enough to embarrass Harvey, but enough to remind Rick. He wasn't getting this all his own way. "Maybe you are at that, Mr Peyton. You and your *I can't smell anything* when I commented on the smell of your gin brewing."

Harvey tipped his head to the side. "You're making gin? Cool. Tell you what, I'll teach you how to play my game if you teach me how to make gin."

Rick held out his hand. "Deal, but the secret of its creation goes to the grave with you."

Harvey gripped his hand and shook it, two firm, very adult shakes that made it clear he saw them as equals. "Deal, bro. Sweet! I'm glad to have you home."

Chapter Twenty-Nine

Rick checked the seal on his barrel of gin. Red wax with the imprint of a miniature barred window. He grinned at the joke. Gei wasn't rapt in the name, but The Gin Joint's first brew was ready for bottling.

Scents of juniper and lemon myrtle permeated the air, clinging to his clothes even after he locked the door behind him. There would be no tampering with his brew, no additives to his father's recipe. The gin room was his domain, with Reg's blessing. Rick tucked the key into his pocket and headed back to the winery.

A full moon crested the hill across the valley, silvering the buildings of Thornyhill Farm. The harvest was all in, and pressing was in full swing. But tonight was for celebrating. Ahead of him, Jillian and an army of workers had finished setting out platters for the harvest dinner on long trestle tables above the top rows of vines. Harvey was in conversation with Stacey and a young man who must be her brother, Jonah. Rick had dropped Harvey off earlier on his way over to collect the last of his gear from the shearers' quarters.

With Garrett still in hospital and awaiting trial, the need for nightly patrols had vanished and Rick had moved back home to share their mother's house with his brother. What it lacked in accessibility to Geilis, it made up for in reconnecting with his brother.

Tables decorated with clusters of grape leaves ran in parallel rows. On the middle table, in pride of place, rose an elaborate cake made by Katy to represent a champagne bottle pouring the next Romney vintage into an oversized glass. Impossible as it seemed, the cake bottle appeared to be suspended in mid-air, pouring with no visible means of support. Rick was impressed.

A figure half in shadow beckoned from a spot on the edge of the light. The boots were a dead giveaway. Rick headed over to join his special guest. "Hi, Dad. Glad you decided to come. I've got something for you." Rick doubted the pleasure of that greeting would ever disappear. He reached into his shirt pocket, took out a yellowing envelope and handed it to his father.

"What's this?" Graham turned the envelope over and over in his hands before gingerly lifting the flap and peering inside.

"Your marriage certificate."

Graham frowned and pinned Rick with a strange eagerness in his gaze. "Where did you get this?"

"Mum kept a few items in a safety deposit box at the bank. I have no idea if Garrett knew about you when he married Mum, but he sure as hell knew after she died. She left me the key to the box in her will. Garrett took it and claimed the contents."

His father took out the folded marriage certificate and carefully, almost reverently, opened it. A wedding photo of his parents lay inside, younger than Rick was now and obviously in love. Graham brushed his thumb over the image of his young wife. "She was beautiful, your mother."

"They're yours, Dad. I had a copy made of the photo."

"Thanks." His father folded the certificate around the photo, placed them in the envelope and put the envelope into his shirt pocket. His hand rested over the pocket for a moment, as though holding Rick's mother close.

"I have a question . . . I always thought Peyton was Mum's maiden name, but the certificate shows she was a

Willoughby. Where does Muggeridge come from? Were you hiding in plain sight?"

"Precisely the reason. How could I keep an eye on your mother and live unnoticed and unremarked if everyone in town knew I was your father? I played a mug's game. The name suited." A two-note laugh escaped, rusty through lack of use.

"I'm cool with people knowing you're my father if you ever decide to assume your real name." Rick would be proud to have his father acknowledge their relationship. "But I get it if you want to keep your anonymity."

Stacey and her young brother and Harvey glanced their way and Graham stepped back into the shadows.

"Christ, I feel like the worm in a school of fish." Graham's hand twitched the collar of the shirt Rick had loaned to him.

"We don't bite, I promise." Geilis slipped in on Graham's other side and took his arm. "Lovely to see you here, Graham. Can I get you a beer or a wine, something classy or something long?"

Engaged in conversation with Geilis, Graham seemed not to notice she was drawing him closer to the group where her father stood chatting with Travis and Katy. Reg looked across as they approached.

"Dad, Graham is here."

"Graham, welcome. Long time, no see." Reg held out his hand.

Graham was introduced to others and shook hands around the small group.

Rick drew Geilis aside, leaned close and whispered in her ear. "Neatly accomplished, Ms Romney. Want to help me get a beer for my father?" He twined his fingers with hers and gently tugged her around the corner.

"What—have you got a secret stash hidden away?"

"Maybe—and just maybe I need to get you to myself for a few minutes."

"I can't think why." But as soon as they rounded the corner, Geilis slipped into his arms. Her mouth found his and her lips, warm and tasting of lush Romney Merlot, elicited a deep groan from him.

He held her close, kissing her, needing her. "Gei, come home with me after the party."

"Yes please. Only you'll have to promise to get me back early. The newest director of Romney Wines can't be seen to be slacking off the first morning on the job."

"Me either. The Gin Joint begins bottling tomorrow."

"Is there no way I can convince you to change the name of your gin?"

"I'm open to all forms of bribery, especially if they involve you, naked, in my bed."

She traced a finger down his throat and over the V of skin exposed by his open collar. "I have a feeling nothing will change your mind. But I won't rule out trying any possibility."

He tipped his head to steal another kiss. If he didn't have Geilis' hands all over him—and soon—he was certain he'd self-combust.

From around the corner came the distinctive sound of a spoon tapped on glass and the buzz of conversation died down.

Gei pulled away, grabbed his hand and tugged him back to the party. "Come on, I think Dad's about to make his speech."

Reg stood on the steps leading up to the tasting area. He nodded as he surveyed the crowd. "I want to thank all of you for another wonderful year. We've had an excellent harvest, and Romney Wines is about to produce its best-ever vintage. You'll want to lay down plenty of bottles from this year in your cellar."

Laughter and several 'hear hears' greeted his comments.

"It's been a difficult year for me personally, and an unusual year for the business. But this last year has also been a year of growth, and change. Romney Wines is heading in a new direction. Geilis is joining Jillian and I as an equal partner in the business—and, might I add, she'll be the managing partner as of tomorrow. Jill and I are going to do lots more travelling."

Enthusiastic clapping and a loud, sustained whistle revealed a strong level of support for the news. Rick slipped his arms around Geilis' shoulders and pulled her back against his chest. "I told you—everyone's happy at the news, sweetheart."

Geilis bent her head and kissed his forearm.

Reg held up his hand and the clapping abated. "In addition, Rick Peyton is joining us as an affiliated business with The Gin Joint, which also opens for business tomorrow. Bush-inspired gins will be sold alongside Romney wines through our cellar door."

More applause, genuine and as loud as that given to Geilis made Rick feel like a new chapter had opened for him, one in which he was a free man, without the stigma of the criminal charges now his stepfather had confessed to setting Rick up.

Anything's possible. Everything is possible now.

"I'd like you to raise your glasses in a toast—to Geilis Romney, new managing partner, and to Rick Peyton. Long may their partnership last."

"Amen to that." Graham stood beside them, his glass raised. "I'm happy being your silent partner, son, but don't expect me to get up and talk like that—ever."

"I won't, Dad." Rick looked at the father he'd so recently found, a man so honourable he'd given up the woman he loved when he'd been unable to care for her. He looked at the woman who'd believed in him in spite of who she thought he was, a woman who'd been prepared to take a chance on him. Like his mother had with his father. "Cheers, Gei. Here's to our partnership."

She tapped her bottle against his. "Bet you never imagined saying that when you started working here."

"Two months ago, I couldn't imagine most of what's happened, but I'll be forever grateful you gave me a chance."

"Thank my father. He's the one who insisted we needed you. He's always been able to pick the best of the bunch. Get it?"

"Are you going to keep on with the bad puns?"

"Only until you find a way to stop me." Gei wrinkled her nose at him and blew him a kiss.

"I have the perfect solution just as soon as we get home."

Gei leaned her head on his shoulder and looked up, a glimmer of laughter in her eyes. "I like the sound of that. Just don't ever call our home, The Gin Joint."

"Never. Home is a perfectly good word. Home is spelled G-E-I-L-I-S."

THE END

Read on for tasters of other books and how to connect with me!

About Susanne Bellamy

Born and raised in Toowoomba, Susanne is an Australian author of contemporary and rural romances set in Australia and exotic locations. She adores travel with her husband, both at home and overseas, and weaves stories around the settings and people she encounters. Her Outback series, *Hearts of the Outback,* was inspired by her time teaching in far north-west Queensland.

Her heroes have to be pretty special to live up to her real life hero. He saved her life then married her. They live on the edge of the Range with their German Shepherd, Freya. In another life, Susanne was a senior English and Drama teacher with a passion for Shakespeare and creative writing, but now her two children have flown the coop, she writes full time.

Susanne is a member of the RWA (Romance Writers of Australia). A hybrid author, she is published with Harlequin Escape and Mira, as well as being self-published. A popular guest speaker, she presented the keynote address at the Steele Rudd Pilgrimage, and was a guest speaker for the Dynamic Life Series for U3A, and has been invited to speak in libraries, at book clubs, and to community groups.

I hope you enjoyed book 2 in Home to Lark Creek! If you would like to share the love and leave a review, I would be grateful.

Here's a taster of my Outback series, *Hearts of the Outback.*

Just One Kiss: http://bit.ly/1Oq3KAX

Chapter One

"The horses are at the barrier . . . and *they're off and racing* in the Cloncurry Stakes. Big Mike takes an early lead but the favourite, Jester, is . . ." The race caller's excited voice blurred amid cheers from the crowd thronging the remote north-west Queensland racecourse.

Dr Dan Middleton glanced at the red dirt track and the dust cloud lazily settling over the race day crowd. Women dressed as smartly as those at Flemington on Cup Day teetered on high heels on hard-packed earth. If there were a few more plastic cups of beer than flutes of champagne, the effect was much the same.

He swallowed the last of his beer and swatted at the flies hovering near his mouth. Horses thundered around the final bend and the crowd surged towards the barriers. A whirly-wind picked up dust, swirling and tracking behind a slim, young woman, the only other racegoer not focused on the race. Caught unawares by the sudden gust, she turned her back and struggled to hold her hat and dress as it lifted in the wind. Her pink dress ballooned and flipped up like one of his mother's fuschias. Tanned legs went all the way up to a pair of silky white panties and Dan grinned.

As suddenly as it had risen, the wind dropped. The woman exhaled and swatted dust from her full skirt. Twitching the outfit into place, she continued towards the beer tent. And Dan.

Faint pink flared in her cheeks as her gaze connected with his and he realised he was still ogling her and grinning.

"Perv." She pushed past him, knocking the plastic cup out of his hand.

By the time he retrieved it and stood, she had disappeared into the crowd around the bar.

"Great way to make an impression, doc." Mark Rogers, a

mechanic with the Royal Flying Doctor Service in Mt. Isa, raised his cup in a mock salute.

"Bad timing. Story of my life." How could he have let himself forget the perils of showing his appreciation of the female form? Surely he'd learned that lesson by now?

"How so, doc? Thought you'd have nurses hanging off your arm. Besides, our Amy's a pretty girl and—"

"Drop it, Mark. Not interested." Dan couldn't afford to be. As much as his job with the Royal Flying Doctor Service let him follow his passion for rural medicine, like his mother and grandfather before him, it was an opportunity to get away from the mud slinging. Although he was pleased his staff at Gosford Hospital had told the truth and stood up for him. And now—

"Don't say that too loud. People might think you're—"

"Gay?" he finished off for the burly mechanic.

"So you're not interested in Amy? She'll be relieved to hear that."

"I'm here to work. That's all. Why?"

"You're rostered on together. She's your pilot."

##

Amy Alistair peered into the small mirror in the ladies loo. Dust caked her face and her cleavage itched, and her new dress had acquired an unflattering layer of red that even the drycleaner would struggle to remove.

And her last-in-the-field horse was probably still running, which was why she'd been heading to the beer tent when the willy-willy sent her skirt flying and Mr Smug and Brooding had copped an eyeful.

Along with half the male population of town.

He'd been the first male she encountered after the wind caught her unawares, and maybe she'd overreacted but his amusement had ratcheted up her embarrassment and her temper had run away with her. Dull red had stained his cheeks as he bent to pick up the cup she'd knocked out of his hand.

She almost felt sorry for him. Until Mechanic Mark nudged him and nodded in her direction. Slinking behind two burly blokes propping up the bar, she sought a safe, non-windy corner where she could quietly sink into the floor. Thank goodness she'd be back in the Isa tomorrow and could get back into work trousers.

Sharyn, her nemesis at high school and all-round stuck-up prig since she'd won Miss North West Queensland, popped her head around the entrance and chuckled. "Hey, Amy, nice knickers. Didn't realise you were so hard up for a date that you'd flash everyone. But hey, you got the eye of the new hottie." With a snort, Sharyn waved her mobile phone and withdrew.

Damn the two-second rule. If Sharyn had seen Amy's awkward moment, the whole region would know by—Amy checked her watch—now.

Oh, hell, had Sharyn got photos too?

Amy cruised along the strip of highway back to the Isa, her iPod on shuffle. As her red ute crested a slight rise, the headlights caught on metallic silver paint and flashing hazard lights. She eased back on the accelerator and pulled in behind a car with its bonnet raised. Someone had left the races earlier than her, it seemed. And by the large dent in the bonnet, they'd encountered a roo on the highway back to Mt. Isa.

She switched her lights to low beam and stepped out of her ute. The driver appeared around the front of the car, holding a torch in one hand and shading his eyes with the other.

"Well, if that doesn't put the icing on this day." She bit her lip, hoping her muttered comment hadn't carried to the man.

"Thanks for stopping. I've lost a headlight and—" Mr Smug and Brooding stopped as she walked past the front of her car. Of course it had to be him broken down at the side of the road. She contemplated jumping back in her ute and hightailing it. For all of five seconds.

"Yeah, well, let's see how bad the damage is." Even to her own ears, her voice sounded snarky. But dammit, she'd bought a new dress and that stupid hat and even crammed her feet into high heels for the racing carnival in celebration of her promotion.

Stupid choice. When did any male look at Amy Alistair with

more than friendship on his mind? She was one of the boys, not tall and elegant like Sharyn.

She held out her hand for his torch, stalked around to the front of his car and peered under the hood. With an ease born of familiarity with machinery on the family property, she assessed the damage. "Your radiator's taken a beating as well as the bonnet. I doubt it will get you to Mt. Isa tonight. You do know you can't drive over eighty on these roads after dusk?"

"I doubt I was doing even that. The roo was going faster than me." Annoyance tinged his voice and he shoved his hands into his pockets. "Any chance I can catch a lift with you?"

The last thing Amy wanted was this prig invading her space. But leaving him by the side of the road waiting for another ride wasn't an option. She wouldn't leave her worst enemy in such a fix, and he was far from that. Even if he had smirked at her *wardrobe malfunction*. She shuddered as she imagined the phrase with Sharyn's intonation. "Hop in."

"Thank you." Stiff formality crackled in those two words.

Amy sniffed and thumbed the torch off. Let him be in a snit. Maybe he wouldn't want to talk as they drove, and that would suit her fine.

##

Dan reached into the boot for his medical bag. He needed travelling with the belligerent blonde like he needed a hole in the head. Petite and feisty, she clearly didn't want his company. Maybe Amy had been given the lowdown on him already. If his reason for leaving Gosford had been leaked to his new employer, he could hardly begin with a clean slate. The thought depressed him before he remembered her obvious embarrassment at the races.

A memory of white silk and tanned thighs rushed back as he thought of their unfortunate meeting, and he slammed the boot. Thank God she didn't realise how clearly her ute's lights had outlined her curves as she'd approached him. High heels had been replaced by a pair of unlaced work boots but headlights through her filmy skirt revealed far more than swirling wind. Better not share that titbit or she'd order him out of her car. Being stranded sucked, especially when he had several articles he needed to read before reporting for work tomorrow.

He climbed into the cabin and put his bag on the floor. Turning to her, he waited until she was seated and reached for her seatbelt. "I'm Dan. And you're Amy?"

"S'pose Mark told you. I'm surprised you noticed my face."

"Look, I'm sorry I laughed. I didn't intend to embarrass you." Another woman would have laughed off the incident, or played it up. Amy's response suggested she lacked confidence.

Not his problem.

In the soft glow of the dashboard light, her chin tipped higher and her knuckles tightened on the wheel. "Can we not mention that again?" She pulled out onto the highway.

"Consider the subject closed." But Amy was mistaken if she thought he'd forget her. He folded his arms across his chest and closed his eyes.

Thirty minutes later, lulled by the motion of the car and several poor nights' sleep, Dan woke with a start as Amy pulled into the first service station on the way into town. He sat up and rubbed the back of his neck.

"I've got to pick up a few groceries. Where do you want me to drop you off?" She opened her door and jumped out before turning and pinning him with her hazel gaze.

"Uh, I can catch a taxi from here."

Amy nodded, rummaged in the side pocket of the door and took out a business card, which she passed across the centre console. "If you're sure. That's for a towing company. Ask Derro to organise a tow for your car in the morning. Night."

Dan looked at the card before opening his door. "Thanks for the ride." He shoved the card in his shirt pocket, grabbed his bag and made for the taxi rank across the side street without looking back.

Under other circumstances, he might have asked Amy out to dinner. Just to say thanks. But she'd made it clear she didn't want to see him again. Which would make tomorrow very interesting.

Do you like your stories with a twist of suspense?

Read on for an introduction to *High Stakes*, a romantic suspense set on the track to Mt Everest in Nepal.

Prologue

Sydney, Australia

John Chan faced his father across the antique rosewood desk. Eyes black and lustreless as coal pinned him to the parquet floor. Sleek, satin lapels contrasted with his snow-white tuxedo, and the benign smile he'd bestowed on guests gathered to celebrate his birthday in the marquee below was wiped from his face. Loss of face, especially for the eldest son of the head of family, was unacceptable. He bowed his head and waited for his father to pronounce sentence.

"You allowed her into your office because you let desire for this woman overrule your head. The woman accessed your computer. She escaped. We may be compromised."

"Father, I regret—"

"For a woman." Disgust leached through his words, pitching his voice higher than normal.

It didn't matter that John had increased profits since taking over operations in Sydney. Endangering the family and the business meant his life was forfeit. If his father so wished.

"Third Uncle wants your balls stuffed in your mouth. Second Uncle prefers a visit to the shark tank."

Of course. A bullet to his temple would be considered weakness.

Bile rose in John's throat. Hands gripped tightly together, he tried to swallow the lump of fear threatening to block his response. Now was not the time to show emotion. Now was the time for quick thinking, and for negotiation. What could he offer in exchange for his life?

"I have a contact in the Bureau. May I protect my family by accessing my resources?"

His father shifted on his seat. Red and gold brocade rustled, and shimmered in the low light preferred by his ageing eyes. He tapped one gnarled index finger on the wooden arm of the chair. When it stopped, John raised his eyes to meet his father's.

"Do this, and perhaps your uncles and I will let you live." His father dismissed him with a single flick of his hand. As though he was no more than a fly.

The woman he had sought to win as his mistress had brought him to this.

Anger seared his gut as John bowed and backed out of his father's office. Luxury and all the clothes wealth could afford had been offered but the woman had played him for a fool. Humiliation would be heaped on her tenfold. She would pay dearly.

He pulled his phone from his pocket and unlocked it with his thumbprint. Scrolling through his contacts, the tremor in his fingers filled him with shame. When the code name appeared, he stabbed the screen and waited. Hand in pocket, he peered through the window. Rivulets of rain blurred his view of the formal garden, and red Poinciana leaves bled into a green bush.

The connection rang four times, as it always did. "What do you want now? I told you, she went to the airport where our tail lost her."

His contact had never shown him respect. One day, when his usefulness was over, John would take pleasure in putting a bullet into Iceman's brain.

But not yet.

"You have one chance. Find her. Kill her."

Chapter One

Jake Harris crossed his scuffed trekking boots and touched his

SUSANNE BELLAMY

whisky glass to the UN commissioner's. Damn if the man didn't keep the best supply this side of Everest. He sipped, welcoming the burn of island peat on his tongue, down his throat, in his gut. Not one drop had touched his lips in two months. Not since he'd found his brother in the garage.

Hanging like a frozen side of beef.

Dead.

The memory slammed through him with the force of an avalanche, and the whisky soured in the black pit of his soul.

Peter. Baby brother. Coke-head.

Dead.

He set the crystal tumbler on the mahogany desk with a thunk. Lamplight lit the lower half of his body and he leaned back, praying his face was in deep shadow. If—when—he got his hands on those responsible for Pete's death, he'd bring them down. By any means. "What do you need from me, Mr Nicholls?"

Grey jacket sleeves rode up and revealed pristine white cuffs. The commissioner folded soft hands on the desk, and his socially-polite, upwardly-mobile smile, the smile of the career diplomat, was packed away. "I understand you're a man of few words. I suppose that's why you chose field work over the diplomatic corps."

The commissioner's plummy tones grated. Jake preferred lilting Nepalese voices to Oxford city-slickness. "I'm leaving Kathmandu in the morning."

"Impatient, Mr Harris?"

"I have new field agents to train." In truth, his second-in-charge in the south-east Asia division of the Bureau was responsible for inductions, but Jake needed space. Room to breathe, open air, and pushing himself to the limit so he could snatch a few hours of dreamless sleep. So far the plan had failed more than it had succeeded.

"Fine, let's cut to the chase. Doctor Westcott is heading up the trail towards Everest Base Camp. Ostensibly on holiday." Nicholls drew a folder towards him.

"And?"

"It's the second part of her trip we hold concerns about."

"Congratulations on solving all the major world problems." He didn't bother trying to subdue his sarcastic side. Sarcasm was good. Sarcasm masked his I'm-going-through-hell face and made taking his next breath, and the next, and the next, possible.

Bitter sarcasm was all he had left.

Because he'd failed. Failed to protect one of the few people he cared about.

Nicholls' hooded eyes fixed on Jake and the sharp plane of his nose lowered as if he were a bird dropping from the sky on hapless prey. Jake glared right back at the commissioner and to hell with protocol. He didn't give a damn if he pissed the man off. He didn't give a damn about anything.

Nicholls fiddled with the knot of his tie. "Doctor Westcott has applied for a research permit to visit the Dolpa region." Jake flicked through memories of his only trip to the central province. "It's remote, difficult to access, and entry permits are expensive and restricted. Not many trekkers go there. What's the concern?"

"Her specialty. Biological chemistry."

"So? I don't see the connection."

Nicholls leaned back and a smug smile tugged at the corners of his mouth. "Need to know basis, Harris."

Jake thought about telling Nicholls to take his intrigue and shove it where the sun didn't shine. The words teetered on the springboard of his tongue, raw, harsh, bitter. He couldn't give a flying fuck. Not when he had a mountain of paperwork, and a group of raw recruits to whip into shape. "I'm head of drug enforcement operations for the region. Who the hell do you think needs to know if not me?"

Nicholls pursed his lips and tapped his fingers on the closed folder. "This case requires top security clearance."

"Which I have. So—she's a biological chemist. What's the connection?"

"Her work involves research and synthesising compounds."

"Making what? Who for, and why here?"

"That's the problem; we don't know."

"Is Doctor Westcott flying in or trekking?"

Nicholls' internal struggle—to stand firm or answer—drew twin lines of battle between his eyebrows. "What difference does it make?"

A flicker of pleasure licked through Jake. Poncy desk jockey didn't know everything. "Have you ever trekked, Mr Nicholls?"

"Not really my cup of tea." Nicholls' clipped tone dismissed the absurd notion. He picked up a pen and patterned the print label on the folder in a series of jabs. The pen stopped, point down amid a mess of blue dots.

"Why is her mode of travel important?" The question was dragged from him like a dentist pulling a bad tooth.

Jake reached for his glass and took a leisurely mouthful. Nicholls' ignorance of transport within Nepal betrayed his inexperience, but it gave Jake the edge to prise out more details about the woman.

"How she travels determines how much and what can be carried. Unless I know more about what I'm meant to be looking for, I can't help you." He tossed back the last mouthful of whisky. "That's a smooth drop. Don't mind if I have another." Warmth spread through his belly and he poured two fingers' into his glass and sat back.

An antique clock chimed the quarter hour and the echoes hung heavily as Nicholls appeared to deliberate. Finally, he spoke. "Drugs."

The single word blazed like a neon light in the night. Jake's breath caught on the sharp rock of grief lodged in his throat, his stomach clenched. His hands fisted on his knees, and a bongo-beat accelerated in his brain: *Revenge—Peter—revenge—Peter—revenge.*

"You were instrumental in breaking up an international supply line out of Afghanistan last month. I believe the leader, Al-Kohari was killed?"

"Yes." The word shot out like the bullet that put the drug lord beyond reach of justice. The legal kind, at least. Jake's only regret was Al-Kohari had been the key to finding and proving the Australian connection. Without him ...

Nicholls leaned back. "Nepal isn't exactly drug territory but if

Doctor Westcott is involved, we need to know."

"If she's involved, I'll bring her in."

Nicholls capped the pen. "The doctor dined with John Chan in Sydney a few days before she arrived in Kathmandu. Chan is the eldest son of a family with Asian drug links. He met the doctor at an upmarket restaurant on Sydney's Circular Quay."

Jake's heart stuttered then began a mad thumping. The Chan cartel was likely Peter's supplier. He could still see his younger brother's face, purple and obscene above the noose. Jake forced his lungs to breathe. His hand clenched the glass and he downed the whisky in a single mouthful.

"This was taken by an undercover agent tailing Chan." Nicholls opened the folder and handed over an enlarged photo.

Beneath heavy, long, black curls, the woman's delicate expression appeared intent on her dinner companion. She was beautiful. His dispassionate gaze began cataloguing details; from the tilt of her head to the thigh-high slit in her black dress, sex appeal oozed from the woman.

"You said she was dining with Chan. Do you think it was business or pleasure?" Jake tipped the photo towards the desk lamp. "Have you got a magnifier?"

Nicholls took an old-fashioned magnifying glass from his drawer and handed it across the desk. "By the look of her I'd say pleasure, but this was the only time the operative saw them alone together."

Jake examined the photograph closely, paying attention to a mark on the woman's thigh, visible in the thigh-split of the slim-fitting black dress.

A tattoo. Maybe a snake or a gecko. He studied her features, memorising them. Any link to the Chans ensured he would take on this assignment. "So how does her trip to Dolpa fit in with this Sydney drug cartel?"

"We suspect a connection. Her visa states the trip is for research. Loopholes in the laws of both our countries allow the legal importation of certain *natural* drugs, which are then recombined. Some of the ingredients in recombined form are responsible for the recent spate of deaths in your capital cities. And mine."

Jake set the photo and magnifier on the desk. "The Chans are at the centre of it?"

"In Sydney, almost certainly."

"Paul Rimmer and I worked undercover in Sydney before I was promoted to head up the Asian bureau. At last contact, he hinted he was onto someone involved in the local trade."

And now Nicholls was handing him a connection to that underworld family. If it was the last thing he did he would find this woman who had allied herself with the Chinese drug cartel and he would extract the truth. And if she was involved in manufacturing and research . . . Jake's hand fisted on his knee.

"Too many young lives are being cut short." Nicholls' comment lacked real emotion. But bureaucratic say-the-right-thing blah hit Jake hard.

Peter would never grow up, grow old, grow anything. He had ceased to exist except in Jake's memory, and as a black and white statistic on a government department's page.

Grief sank in Paul's gut like a boulder, free-falling down—down—down—into a bottomless chasm.

But he couldn't afford the luxury of time to grieve. Time in which the drug family would set up a new supplier, find new supply lines, shatter more families. He pulled himself together, locked his grief down tighter than an airport on terrorist alert. Peter's death would not go unavenged.

"So this doctor is working for the cartel?"

"That, Harris, is what we want you to find out. Observation only for the time being, but we want to know what the Dolpa connection is. If you confirm a link to the Chans, bring her in." Nicholls closed the folder and shoved it across the desk. "We want eyes on her as soon as possible, before she makes contact with anyone. How quickly can you reach Everest Base Camp?"

"I'll fly in by helicopter tomorrow and backtrack until I find her. Before she reaches Everest, I'll catch her."

And if the doctor was working for the drug family, he would make her pay.

You can find the book here: <u>http://amzn.to/2Ek44Y4</u>

Acknowledgements:

As always, many thanks to my editor and critique partner, Annie Seaton, for her support, enthusiasm and guidance, and to Caitlin Rees and Erin Moira O'Hara for critiques and proof reading. You make my work shine!

You can find me at the following:

a. Facebook
   <u>https://www.facebook.com/susanne.bellamy.7</u>

b. Twitter
   <u>https://twitter.com/SusanneBellamy</u>

c. Website   <u>http://www.susannebellamy.com/</u>

d. Pinterest
   <u>http://www.pinterest.com/susannebellamy/</u>

e. Bookbub
   <u>https://www.bookbub.com/profile/susanne-bellamy?list=about</u>

f. Goodreads
   https://www.goodreads.com/author/list/6869630.Susanne_Bellamy

Or on my website: http://www.susannebellamy.com

www.ingramcontent.com/pod-product-compliance
Lightning Source LLC
Chambersburg PA
CBHW030642110726
47901CB00002B/538